P9-CLB-604

OTHERWOOD

PETE HAUTMAN

CANDLEWICK PRESS

This is a work of fiction. Names, characters, places,
and incidents are either products of the author's
imagination or, if real, are used fictitiously.

Copyright © 2018 by Pete Hautman

All rights reserved. No part of this book may be reproduced, transmitted,
or stored in an information retrieval system in any form or by any means,
graphic, electronic, or mechanical, including photocopying, taping,
and recording, without prior written permission from the publisher.

First edition 2018

Library of Congress Catalog Card Number pending
ISBN 978-0-7636-9071-7

18 19 20 21 22 23 LSC 10 9 8 7 6 5 4 3 2 1

Printed in Crawfordsville, IN, U.S.A.

This book was typeset in Dante MT.

Candlewick Press
99 Dover Street
Somerville, Massachusetts 02144

visit us at www.candlewick.com

MIX
Paper from
responsible sources
FSC
www.fsc.org   FSC® C132124

For the children and the foxes
of Bone Woods

Is reality simply a dream we share?
Will sharing my story change what is real?
Alas, I will never know.

—*Book of Secrets*

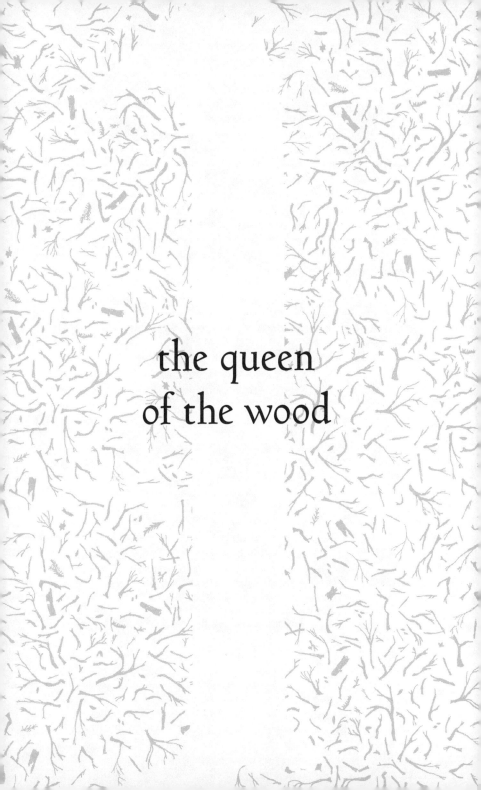

the queen
of the wood

the storm

Years later, people still talked about it.

It came out of nowhere, they said.

Middle of the day.

Black as night.

Sideways rain.

Trees bent and twisted like blades of grass.

Stuey had been just eight years old, but he remembered the storm as if it were yesterday.

Thunder you could feel in your belly.

"Everybody in the basement! Now!" his mom shouted.

Grandpa Zach rushed outside to close the windows on his writing cottage.

"Daddy!" Stuey's mom called after him.

"I'll be fine," Grandpa Zach yelled back. He ducked into the cottage just as the first hailstones came hammering down. A clap of thunder left Stuey's ears ringing. His mom slammed the door and hustled him downstairs to the basement.

"Grandpa will wait out the storm in his cottage, Stuey," she told him shakily. "He'll be okay."

When the thunder finally stopped, Stuey and his mom came up from the basement. Outside, it looked like another world. Trees stripped bare. Grass littered with leaves, twigs, and shingles. Melting hailstones big as fists. Hundreds of sheets of yellow paper scattered everywhere.

The roof of the guest cottage was gone, torn off by the wind.

They found Grandpa Zach on the floor behind his desk, curled up, arms wrapped around his belly as if he was hugging himself. Around him were scattered yellow pages covered with his handwriting, his crabbed and spidery script bleeding from the rain.

Gramps's eyes were open, staring sightlessly at the sodden pages. Wet gray hair straggled across his cheek.

"Stuey, go back to the house," his mother said.

"Why?"

"Just go."

Stuey remembered that day the way he remembered nightmares—a sort of horrific slide show, one awful image piled on top of another. He went back to the house, carrying with him the knowledge that Gramps, his best friend, was gone. The shock was so sudden and complete that he couldn't even cry. He didn't cry then, nor at Grandpa Zach's funeral three days later.

He couldn't bear to touch the emptiness.

According to the news, it hadn't been a tornado but straight-line winds with multiple downbursts—angry clouds firing air cannons at the ground. The cottage had taken a direct hit.

Half a mile away, in the middle of Westdale Wood, a second downburst had toppled five tall cottonwoods to create an enormous deadfall, but no one had been there to see it.

2
creepy bent

The day before the storm, Stuey had discovered the fairy circle.

Stuey lived with his mom and Gramps at the end of Ford Lane, in the largest and oldest home in Westdale, a three-story house so big they used only half the rooms. The house was gray. Battleship gray, Gramps called it. Stuey's bedroom was on the third floor overlooking their small apple orchard.

Their house had been built by Stuey's great-grandfather. Stuey's mom had grown up there. Grandpa Zach had lived there his whole life.

The other six houses on Ford Lane were newer, normal-size homes on smaller lots. There were no kids his age. Stuey's best friend, Jack Kopishke, had moved away last summer.

With nobody in the neighborhood to play with, Stuey mostly hung around with his mom and Gramps, or went off by himself to explore.

On the far side of the orchard was a meadow, and beyond the meadow was Westdale Wood—one square mile of towering oaks, wildflower-carpeted glades, glossy waist-high stands of poison ivy and mayapple, prickly tangles of gooseberry, nettles, burdock, blackcaps, raspberries, and wild grape. There were deer and rabbits and wild turkeys, raccoons and foxes and mink. Butterflies and hornet nests. Cicadas and mosquitoes. Boggy places that would suck the shoes off your feet. Mossy, boulder-strewn ravines. Impenetrable thickets of buckthorn. Stuey had explored only a small part of it. He had never been to the other side.

That morning, while Gramps was in his cottage writing and his mom was in her studio painting, Stuey wandered off through the apple orchard. The apples were tiny green nubbins. Most of them would be wormy when they got bigger. Gramps didn't believe in spraying the trees. "Bugs have to eat too," he liked to say. When autumn arrived they would salvage enough good apples for the three of them.

Stuey crossed the orchard and waded through the tall grasses of the meadow. On the far side of the meadow stood a grove of white-barked poplar trees. Stuey usually avoided the poplar grove—the trees grew too close together, and the gaps between them were choked with underbrush. But on that day he noticed a narrow deer path leading into the grove, so he followed it. He had gone only a few yards when he came upon a treeless circle of grass.

The circle was about thirty feet across and brilliant green. The grass hugged the ground, as if someone had been mowing it. Stuey dropped to his knees and ran his hands over the velvety surface.

He stood up and walked across the circle. His faint footprints lasted only a few seconds before the tiny blades of grass sprang back to erase them. He looked around at the ring of tall, slender poplars pressing in as if they were spectators.

It felt magical.

Stuey left the grove and ran back to Gramps's writing cottage. The old man was hunched over his desk, puffing on his pipe and filling another yellow page with his memories. Even though it was a warm summer day he was wearing the ratty wool cardigan he called his "smoking sweater."

"Gramps, come see! I found a fairy circle!"

"A fairy circle, you say?" Grandpa Zach capped his fountain pen.

"In the poplar grove!"

"Fairies in the poplars?" He chuckled.

"Come see!"

Grandpa Zach tapped the ashes out of his pipe and set it on his pipe stand. He pressed both hands on his desk and stood up. He adjusted his sweater and his saggy gray pants.

"Fairies in the poplars," he said again, shaking his head. "What'll they think of next?"

Stuey led him out of the cottage and across the meadow to the poplars. He had to stop and wait a few times because Gramps was really slow. They followed the path into the grove and came to the circle of green.

Grandpa Zach laughed, and his laugh turned into a cough, as it often did. He cleared his throat and said, "It's an old golf green, Stuey. The tenth hole, if I'm not mistaken. This whole woods used to be a golf course, you know."

"I know, you've told me: 'The biggest and best golf course in the state.'"

"That's right. Built by your great-grandfather. My pop."

Grandpa Zach's father, Stuart Ford, had built Westdale Country Club back in the 1930s. Rich people from Minneapolis and Saint Paul would drive their fancy cars to play Westdale's tree-lined fairways, its suede-smooth greens, its white-sand bunkers. Gramps had told that story often. But the golf course closed a few years after World War II.

"There were twenty-seven greens like this back in the day, but I imagine the rest have all been overgrown. Out in those woods you might still find a few patches here and there." Grandpa Zach bent down and ran his hand over the grass. "This is a special kind of grass called creeping bent."

"Creepy bent?"

"*Creeping* bent."

"I like *creepy* bent better," Stuey said.

"It *is* a little creepy." Gramps stood up, knees cracking, and regarded the white-barked trees surrounding them. "It's almost as if they're protecting the green. Poplars like sandy soil, and this green was once surrounded by sand traps — Pop always called them bunkers. You dig down under these trees and you'll find pure white sand trucked all the way from New Mexico."

He shook his head sadly and looked down at the soft green carpet beneath his feet. "Now the woods are devouring the past. When I was not much older than you, I used to practice my putting here."

Stuey pictured Gramps as a boy, standing on this very place. It was so far away, yet so close and real it sent a shiver up his spine.

"Times change, Stuey. Before it was a golf course, this was a marsh. You know Barnett Creek? Just north of the highway?"

Stuey nodded. He and Jack Kopishke had caught crayfish and tadpoles there.

"Well, there used to be a branch of the creek that flowed south. Where we're standing now was all water, mud, and cattails. Pop dammed up the south fork back in the thirties and drained the land on this side of the highway. He built our house, and Westdale Country Club." He looked around with a wistful expression. "I don't believe there are any fairies here, Stuey. But there might be a ghost or two."

"Ghosts?" Stuey's voice quavered. He didn't really believe in fairies, but he wasn't so sure about ghosts.

Grandpa Zach grinned. "Got you!" he said.

Stuey grinned back, relieved and feeling kind of silly. Gramps liked to kid around. But suddenly the old man's smile collapsed and he looked away.

"Do you know what ghosts are, Stuey? I'll tell you.

They're secrets haunting the memories of the living. So long as we carry their secrets, they refuse to leave. They wait."

"Wait for what?"

"To be forgotten. My father has been gone sixty years, but"—he tapped the side of his head—"he's still here. He never left."

bootlegger

That night at dinner, Grandpa Zach drank a bottle of beer. He didn't drink beer often, but when he did, he always ended up talking about the old days.

"Back in the twenties," he said, "your great-grandfather was a bootlegger."

"Is that like a pirate?" Stuey asked.

"More like a smuggler," Grandpa Zach said. "Alcohol was illegal back then — this was during Prohibition. Pop was sneaking whiskey over the border from Canada. Everybody knew he was doing it, but the old man was smart. He never got caught."

Stuey's mom said, "Daddy, are you sure you want to drag out our family's dirty laundry?"

"It was a long time ago," Grandpa Zach said.

"Not long enough." Stuey's mom stood up and began clearing the table.

"So, my great-grandpa was a criminal?" Stuey said.

"Well . . . technically, yes. But when Prohibition ended he got out of the smuggling business and went legit. He used his money to build Westdale Country Club. Chances are the golf course would still be there, but one night, just before sunset, Pop was out on the course playing a few holes all by himself, and he disappeared into thin air."

"Disappeared?" Stuey stared wide-eyed, looking for a sign that he was kidding.

"Daddy!" Stuey's mom came back in from the kitchen. "You'll give him nightmares!"

"No he won't," Stuey said.

Grandpa Zach chuckled, then coughed. He took a sip of water, cleared his throat, and waited for her to go back to the kitchen with another armload of dishes. As soon as she left he leaned closer to Stuey.

"He disappeared, Stuey. And he wasn't the only one. A man named Robert Rosen disappeared that same night."

"Was Robert Rosen a bootlegger too?"

"No. Robert Rosen was a lawyer."

"My dad was a lawyer."

"There are lots of different kinds of lawyers." He glanced toward the kitchen. "Your father was a corporate lawyer. Robert Rosen was a district attorney. He chased after criminals, and he'd been after your great-grandfather for years. Rosen claimed that Pop was still a crook, but he could never prove it.

"Their legal battle went on for years. Most everybody in Westdale loved your great-grandfather. He was a real charmer. He gave big donations to all the local causes. He turned a mosquito-ridden marsh into the most beautiful golf course in the state. But a few people resented him because of his past—they thought he was just a crook with money. That was what Robert Rosen thought. Then, that one night, both of them disappeared."

"What happened to them?"

"Nobody knows. Rosen's wife said he'd gone to the club to talk to my father. His car was parked at the clubhouse, and one of the groundskeepers said he saw Rosen walking out onto the course. Some said that Pop murdered Rosen, buried the body, and ran off to Mexico. Others said the opposite. All we know for sure is that neither of them was ever seen again."

"What do *you* think happened?"

He shook his head slowly. "I was only seventeen then, just a kid. I used to imagine he was out there someplace, looking for a way home. Sometimes even now I feel him looking over my shoulder."

"But why would he want to murder that guy?"

"I'm not saying he did, Stuey. But there was a lot of

bad feeling. Robert Rosen was an educated lawyer from a well-to-do Jewish family back East. Pop never finished high school. He fought his way up from nothing, and sometimes he cut corners. He resented educated people like Rosen, and Rosen had no respect for my dad or what he'd accomplished. It was like they came from different worlds, and neither one of them was willing to accept the other. I think those two men hated each other so bad they just hated themselves out of existence."

Stuey's mom came in and said, "Stuey, don't listen to him."

"Hatred is a powerful force, Annie," Grandpa Zach said. "Hatred combined with lies and secrets can break the world."

"I don't know *what* you're talking about! I think you've been spending too much time on your book. You're just picking at old scabs."

"It's *history*, Annie."

"*Your* history, maybe."

"That's right. And *my* history is *your* history, and your history is Stuey's history." He turned to Stuey, bristly eyebrows coming together over his long nose. "We're all connected. My father might be gone, but he left something of himself behind. You spend enough time out in those woods, you'll see him."

"Stop filling his head with rot, Daddy."

"Don't *Daddy* me, Annie. The dead live on in our memories. I remember the last time I saw my father like it was yesterday. He'll haunt those woods until the day I die. I watched those trees grow up on Pop's grave."

"You mean he's buried in the woods?" Stuey asked.

"Who knows? It's the last place he was ever seen. He might still be floating around out there."

"Is that why the golf course closed? Because of ghosts?"

Grandpa Zach shrugged. "The past doesn't go away just because we want it to. If there *are* ghosts we'd never know it because real ghosts look exactly like real people."

"Have you seen them?" Stuey asked.

Grandpa Zach closed his eyes, and when he opened them he seemed to be staring at something far away. "I've seen people who are gone," he said. "If they weren't ghosts, then I don't know what they were."

"Your grandfather is being ridiculous," said his mother. "There are no ghosts."

The old man's eyes snapped back into focus. He forced an unconvincing smile onto his face.

"Your mother's right, Stuey. There are no ghosts. The golf course closed because Pop spent most of his money building it, and the rest on lawyers defending himself from Robert Rosen. We kept it open for a couple years after Pop disappeared. I think Mother expected Pop to walk in the door at any time with that big smile on his face. Boy, would she have let him have it! But Pop never came back, and there were a lot of debts. In the end, the county took the golf course because we couldn't pay the property taxes. All they let us keep was this house and the ten acres it's sitting on.

"When I was younger I thought that one day I'd make a pile of money and buy the land back. That's what Pop would have wanted—to keep it in the family. Maybe *you* can do that, Stuey."

"I'll be a bootlegger!" That sounded like the coolest thing ever.

"No you won't," his mom said.

"A bootlegger and a murderer!" he said, just to bug her.

"Honey, we don't know that anybody killed anybody," his mom said. "All we have is a sixty-year-old rumor being kept alive by an eighty-year-old crank."

"I'm only seventy-nine," Grandpa Zach muttered.

"Well, you're *acting* like you're six." She picked up their water glasses and went back to the kitchen.

Gramps looked after her and sighed. "I'll always wonder what would have happened if Robert Rosen hadn't followed Pop out onto that golf course that night. Every time we make a decision there's a fork in reality, an infinity of possibilities. There are many worlds, but we can only know the one we live in. Maybe in one world my father killed Rosen, and in another reality it was the opposite. Maybe there are worlds where people are still out there hitting golf balls."

"So nothing is real?" Stuey asked.

"Everything is real. And not real," Grandpa Zach said. "The weatherman says there's a big storm coming tomorrow from the west. Chances are it'll knock down some trees in the woods. If a tree falls and you don't see it or hear it, did that tree really fall? In your reality, the tree still stands until one day you find it lying on the ground. In that moment the known and the unknown become one reality. The tree fell." He chuckled. "That would be a good name for my book: *The Tree Fell*."

Grandpa Zach had been working on his book ever since Stuey could remember, filling sheet after sheet of lined yellow pages.

"It's our history," he had once told Stuey. "Things nobody knows. Things nobody would believe. My *Book of Secrets*."

Stuey and his mom recovered hundreds of those yellow pages after the storm, peeling them off the side of the house, pulling them from apple tree branches, picking them out of bushes and off the grass as far away as the meadow. They dried the pages, but the ink had run and smeared. Most of it was illegible.

"I don't know why we bothered," she said with a sigh. "Daddy always said nobody would want to read it anyway."

"I'd read it," Stuey said.

"Maybe someday."

That meant never. She put the dried pages in a large cardboard box, taped it shut, and carried it upstairs, her clogs going *clunk-ka-clunk* on the steps. She always wore clogs around the house.

Stuey followed her up to Grandpa Zach's bedroom. The room was crowded with mementos of a long life: a sword he had brought back from Morocco, a baseball trophy from high school, and an ancient leather bag of golf clubs that had belonged to his father. The tall bookcase held lots of travel books. Gramps had liked to read about northern Africa, where he'd spent time in the navy. There were also several books with *quantum* in the title. Gramps had been fascinated by quantum physics. He had tried to explain it to Stuey — something about atoms and time and space and how two opposite things could be true at the same time.

We live in different worlds, different realities, Gramps had said.

Was Gramps in a different world now? Was he someplace where he was not dead?

The thought made the back of Stuey's neck prickle.

Next to the bookcase was a stand with Gramps's collection of briar pipes. Stuey could still smell the faint aroma of pipe tobacco. There were framed photos on the walls: Gramps's parents in front of the clubhouse, Gramps in his navy uniform, Gramps with his wife, Lois, the grandmother Stuey never knew. She had died when he was two. Everything in the room had a story. Stuey had heard a lot of them. He wished he could hear more.

When Grandpa Zach had been alive, the room had felt alive. Now it felt dead and brittle, as if an earth tremor or a sudden breeze might collapse it all into dust.

"I don't get why he had to die," Stuey said.

"He was old, Stuey," his mom said. "He had a bad heart, and I guess the storm was too much for it. It was his time."

She set the box of papers on the bed.

"Maybe I'll go through these sometime," she said. "Right now I just can't."

"Me neither," Stuey said as they left the room—but he thought one day he might.

His mom must have heard something in his voice. She gave him a sharp look and said, "I don't want you messing around with your grandfather's things, Stuey." She closed the door and added, "This room is off-limits."

the deadfall

The following summer, on the day before his ninth birthday, Stuey packed a peanut butter sandwich, a box of cranberry juice, and an apple into his backpack. He looked out his bedroom window at the orchard, where Grandpa Zach was buried. He could see the granite headstone poking up through the tall grass. None of the other houses in the neighborhood had a grave in the backyard, but his mom said it was what Gramps would have wanted.

Stuey had never hiked all the way to the other side of the woods. Today, he decided, he would do it. One last adventure before he turned nine. He wished he had someone to go with him, but after Jack had moved away, he didn't have any friends in the neighborhood. He was on his own.

He shrugged on his backpack and went to check on his mom. She was in her painting studio lying on the tattered old sofa staring up at the ceiling. She'd been doing that a lot lately.

Stuey backed out of the room and went outside. The sun was shining above, but it was cloudy to the west.

He circled the crumbling stone foundation of Grandpa Zach's writing cottage. At the gravestone he stopped and remembered Gramps as he had been, smoking his pipe and telling stories about the distant past.

"I'm going all the way to the other side of the woods," Stuey said. He didn't really think Gramps could hear him, but it seemed like a good idea to tell some adult where he was going. His mom would say it was too far, but Gramps would understand.

He headed through the orchard and across the meadow to the poplar grove. He hadn't visited the fairy circle since the time he was there with Gramps.

The circle of green felt smaller. The poplars were moving in. *The woods are devouring the past,* as Gramps had said. Stuey imagined his grandfather as a young man with a putter, trying to knock a ball into a hole. What had happened to the hole? He got down on his hands and knees and crawled around, searching. The grass, still slightly moist with morning dew, felt nice and cool. He soon found a hand-size dimple near the center of the circle. Had this been the hole? If so, it had filled in and the grass had grown over it.

He sat back on his heels and looked around. *If there were such things as ghosts or fairies,* he thought, *this is where they would come.*

It was easy to imagine fairies dancing on this circle of green. Of course there were no such things as fairies. He still hadn't made his mind up about ghosts.

A chipmunk appeared from the hollow of a fallen tree at the edge of the green.

Stuey said, "Hello."

The chipmunk darted back into its hollow.

There were no such things as talking animals either.

"See you later," Stuey said.

From far above came the scolding chatter of a red squirrel. Stuey smiled. He liked animals. He had seen deer, raccoons, foxes, and skunks in the woods. Nothing to be afraid of, although he knew to be careful around skunks.

A cloud crossed the sun. He looked up at the sky. It was still mostly blue, but the clouds were moving in from the west. It looked like rain. He thought about going home, but he'd only just started.

He left the grove and headed deeper into the woods,

up a low ridge and onto the oak knoll that marked the eastern edge of their ten acres.

By the time he came down the far side of the knoll, the clouds had completely covered the sky. He heard the faint patter of raindrops hitting the leaves and branches above. He pushed through a chest-high snarl of gooseberry. The prickly stems tugged at his jeans and T-shirt and scratched his arms. He ran to a grove of larger trees and huddled against the trunk of a basswood.

Raindrops struck the dry leaves and soil with a barely audible hiss, the sort of fine, gentle rain that could last for hours. A faint fog, barely visible, gathered in the low areas. He would be soaked no matter what, so he decided to keep going.

Once he gave himself up to the rain, walking was a pleasure. The wet leaves were silent beneath his feet. Rich, earthy smells rose up from the forest floor.

He came to a large fallen tree and turned right to go around it, but ran into a thick copse of buckthorn and had to go around that too. It was as if the woods was directing him, turning him right and left. He followed a winding deer trail up a rise, then down into a low area where the fog had gathered in a chest-high layer.

Cool mist beaded on his face and arms; it was like walking through a cloud. Tall grasses tugged at his sodden jeans. He had gone only a short distance when a massive, dark shape appeared before him. He stopped, not sure what he was seeing.

He took a few more steps and saw that it was an enormous deadfall. Five trees had fallen against one another to form a teepee shape more than thirty feet high, crowned with a tangle of dead limbs and branches. Their twisted, snarly root-balls were packed with earth and chunks of rock. Ranks of mushrooms sprouted from the trunks.

Stuey circled the deadfall. Something must have happened to make all those trees fall at the same time. He thought about the big storm last summer. The downburst that had ripped the roof off the cottage and killed his grandfather—had the same thing happened here?

He remembered what Gramps had told him:

If a tree falls and you don't see it or hear it, did that tree really fall? In your reality, the tree still stands until one day you find it lying on the ground. In that moment the known and the unknown become one reality. The tree fell.

Were these the trees he had been talking about?

Stuey spotted a gap between two of the trunks. He took off his backpack and, dragging it behind him, wriggled through.

Inside the deadfall was an open space, quiet and dry, about twelve feet across. Above his head the dead branches formed a crude lattice, letting in just enough light to see. In the center of the space was a rectangular slab of rock the size of a mattress, partially buried in the earth. Stuey stepped onto the slab and turned slowly in a circle. He raised his arms over his head and touched the tangled branches above him.

It felt like a church shrunk down to kid size. The stone slab was like an altar, but there were no pews and no people. His own private domain. He sat down on the slab and stretched out on his back. The stone was deliciously cool. Slivers and speckles of gray sky showed through gaps in the branches. The sound of rain felt distant and unreal. He closed his eyes.

The stone beneath him felt alive. He imagined he was in a vessel, a ship made of trees, rising and falling on a gentle sea, driven by wind and magic. He heard distant music playing over faint voices. What were they saying? He listened closely. It sounded like men arguing, but the words were muffled and blurry:

Abblesabbleabblegabblesabbada . . .

Gramps had said that there were ghosts in the woods. Was that what he was hearing?

Abblesabblegabblesa . . .

For a moment he thought he heard Gramps's voice among them.

He opened his eyes and sat up. The voices became the hiss of rain on leaves.

"Grandpa?" he said. There was no echo; the dead

branches swallowed his voice. He turned his head to the side. Wisps of mist had gathered around the stone.

"Grandpa?" He said it louder.

Nothing. Stuey could feel his heart beating. He looked out the opening at the wet, gray woods, then back at the dry stone slab. The mist was gone. He laughed at himself.

"Fairy tales," he said. "You got me again, Gramps."

elly rose

Stuey stayed in the deadfall and waited out the rain. There were three small nooks that looked like places to sit. Two fit him perfectly, one was too tight. He sat in the largest nook and ate his apple and drank his cranberry juice, imagining he was a bootlegger being shipped to Alcatraz. He stood on the stone slab and rode it like a surfboard. One of the branches moved up and down like a lever: up for forward, down for reverse. Eventually the rain stopped. Shards of sunlight sprinkled the stone slab, and the birds began to sing.

It took a while to find his way home. He finally came out of the woods behind the Charlestons', their nearest neighbor. His mom was calling from the orchard. He ran toward her voice.

"I'm here," he yelled back.

She spun and clapped a hand to her heart. "Stuey! Where have you been! Look at you! You're drenched!"

"I was in the woods," Stuey told her.

"I've been calling you!"

"I got kind of lost."

"You've been gone for hours!"

"I'm sorry," Stuey said, even though he wasn't sorry at all.

She looked at him and sighed. "Come on. Let's get you a bath and into some dry clothes. The Frankels have invited us to a barbecue."

"Who are they?"

"Hiram and Maddy Frankel. They moved to Westdale last May. Mr. Frankel is on the preservation society with me."

Stuey's mom had joined the Westdale Preservation Society a few months earlier when the county announced that they were considering selling Westdale Wood to a shopping mall developer.

"The Frankels live on the other side of the woods in the Westdale Hills neighborhood."

"Will there be any other kids there?"

"They have a girl about your age. Her name is Elly Rose."

The Frankels' house backed right up against the opposite side of Westdale Wood, only a mile from Stuey's house, but two miles away by car. There were about twenty people gathered in the fenced backyard, mostly adults: the Charlestons, the Dunphies, the Kimballs, and some people he didn't know. The only kids he saw were the Kimballs' teenage daughter, Teresa, the five-year-old Charleston twins, and a couple of babies.

Mr. Frankel, tending the grill, had incredibly hairy legs. He was wearing an apron with pictures of hot dogs printed on it. Mrs. Frankel wore bright-red lipstick and a black-and-white dress that made her look like a zebra. She talked really loud. Stuey hung back during the greetings, but Mrs. Frankel caught sight of him and let out a squeal.

"This must be Stuart!" She loomed over him, streaming waves of perfume. "Look at that hair! It looks like he's got a haystack on his head."

She reached for him; Stuey ducked back behind his mother. Mrs. Frankel emitted a braying laugh.

"Elly Rose, come meet the Becker boy!"

A girl with curly black hair came over to examine

Stuey, peering into his face with enormous eyes so dark brown they appeared to be all pupil. She was the opposite of his husky, pale, haystack-haired self. Her thin body was all angles and points, and she moved in quick jerks. Stuey thought she looked like an elf.

"Elly Rose, this is Stuart Becker."

"It's just Stuey," Stuey said in a near whisper.

"You can call me Elly," the girl said, "unless it's a formal occasion."

Mrs. Frankel moved on to her next victim. Elly Rose's eyes bored into him. She stepped closer. He felt as if she was looking right through his skin. He looked away.

"You're shy," she said. "But I like your nose."

Stuey had never thought about his nose before. "My nose?"

"It's a button," Elly Rose said. She reached out and touched the tip of his nose. Her mouth twitched to the side in a half smile. "There. Now you're frozen."

"No I'm not," Stuey said, waving his arms to prove it.

"You're boring," Elly said, sticking out her bottom lip.

Stuey saw that he had disappointed her, so he pretended to be frozen. "Can't . . . move," he said in a strangled voice.

"That's better." Elly grinned and touched his nose again. "I have unfrozen you. You are free."

"Thank you," said Stuey.

"My birthday is tomorrow," Elly said. "If you promise not to be boring you can come to my party. I'm going to be nine."

Stuey stared at her in shock.

"My birthday is tomorrow," Stuey said.

"I just said that."

"No, I mean *my* birthday is tomorrow!"

the preservation society

Since they had the same birthday, Elly declared that they should be best friends.

Stuey was startled by the offer.

"Unless you already have a best friend," she said after a moment.

"I used to," he said.

Jack Kopishke had moved away to Des Moines two summers ago. Stuey had friends at school, but they were just school friends, and school was out for the summer. Grandpa Zach had been his best friend after Jack left. Now Gramps was gone.

"But not anymore," he added.

"Then you need a new one," she said.

"Okay." He didn't exactly feel like they were best friends yet, but he was willing to give it a try.

"Maybe we were born at the exact same minute." Elly's eyes widened. "We could be twins! I always wanted to be a twin."

"Where were you born?" he asked.

"In New York."

"We're probably not twins then, because I was born here. Besides, we look really different."

Elly frowned, then brightened. "We could be soul mates!"

"What's a soul mate?" he asked.

"It means we have a special connection and we can't have any secrets from each other," Elly said.

Stuey thought about the deadfall. "I only have one secret," he said.

"What is it?"

"I can't tell you. It's secret. A secret place."

"Where is it?"

Stuey felt himself getting stubborn. "If I told you, it wouldn't be a secret," he said.

Elly stared at him fiercely. "Okay," she said after a moment. "We can still be best friends. But we only get one secret each."

"What's your secret?" he asked.

"I can't tell you."

"If I ever tell you my secret you have to tell me yours."

"Okay, deal. So . . . do you have a dad?"

"I did, but he died in a car accident when I was a baby. Mom and me moved in with my grandpa, but Gramps died too. Just last year. Now it's just me and my mom."

"That's tragic," Elly said.

"It's okay. I never really knew my dad. And Gramps was really old. My mom says it was his time."

Elly was silent for a few seconds, then she said, "I have a cat. His name is Grimpus. He only has one eye."

Stuey looked around. "Where is he?"

"Hiding. He doesn't like people. Except me."

"What color is he?"

"Mostly invisible, but he's gray sometimes too."

Stuey and Elly ate their hamburgers and potato salad at the kids' table, a smaller version of the long picnic table where the adults were gathered. Stuey's mom was talking about how the Westdale Preservation Society was trying to save the woods from developers.

"We don't need another gigantic shopping mall full of trashy gift shops and fast-food joints," his mom was saying.

Stan Kimball spoke up. "Anne, I agree with you that nature is important. That's why Forest Hills Development is promising to preserve part of Westdale Wood as a public park."

"I've seen their proposal," Elly's dad said. He was on the preservation society too. "They're promising to turn ten acres into a glorified picnic area. That means they'll flatten the other five hundred ninety acres! Do you really want to look out your window and see the back end of a megamall?"

Mr. Kimball shrugged. "People have to shop somewhere. I'm sure Forest Hills can come up with a plan that will make everybody happy."

"Or nobody happy," Stuey's mom said.

"What are they talking about?" Elly asked.

"The preservation society," Stuey said.

"Borrrrring!"

"I guess they don't want the woods to turn into a shopping center."

"That won't happen," Elly said.

"How do you know?"

"Because I am the Queen of the Wood, and I won't let them." She leaned closer to Stuey and whispered, "I have magical powers."

Elly's intensity was irresistible. He liked that she was the magical Queen of the Wood, and that she said things out loud that he only let himself imagine.

"I know where there's a fairy circle in the woods," he said.

"What's that?"

"I'll show you sometime."

"I found a turkey nest with eighteen eggs in it."

"Do you go in the woods a lot?"

"All the time," Elly said.

"Me too. I saw a fox once."

"Foxes are my loyal subjects."

"What about raccoons?"

"I don't like them. They tip over our garbage."

The adults were getting louder—especially Stan Kimball.

"I think it's great that you want to save the trees and stuff, but this development could lower property taxes for every one of us, not to mention all the jobs it'll create."

"Doesn't your firm handle real estate and property law, Stan?" said Mr. Frankel.

"What are you suggesting?"

"Your firm *would* pick up a lot of clients, right, Stan?" Mr. Frankel said.

"*Everyone* would benefit! You have to look at the big picture—you can't stop progress!"

"You call tearing down a six-hundred-acre forest *progress*? I call it a travesty."

"Look, Hiram, you can hug all the trees you want, but you have to face reality. What you call a forest I call an overgrown derelict golf course full of mosquitoes and ticks and poison ivy and Lord knows what else. Would you let *your* kid play out there?" He gestured toward the gate leading into the woods.

"As a matter of fact, Stan, I do," said Elly's dad.

"He lets me go in the woods," Elly whispered to Stuey, "but my mom doesn't like it."

"My son plays out there all the time," Stuey's mom said. "Better than having him staring at a screen all day long like some kids." She looked pointedly at Teresa Kimball, who was texting on her cell phone.

Stan Kimball's face and neck had turned red.

"I suppose you'd as soon forage for berries and roots to feed your family, but most people want more. Civilization is happening whether you like it or not!"

"I think his eyeballs might explode," Elly whispered.

Stuey didn't laugh. Stan Kimball scared him, and he didn't like him yelling at his mom.

"Calm down, Stan," said Mr. Frankel. "We're trying to have a meaningful conversation here!"

"Why are they all talking so loud?" Elly said. Stan Kimball was going on about taxes and jobs again.

"I think whoever yells the loudest wins," Stuey said.

Elly Rose said, "Do you want to see my magic swing?"

the ravine

No one noticed them slip away. As soon as Elly closed the back gate behind them, the strident adult voices were replaced by the sounds of birds and wind and shivering leaves. Before them was a broad, descending slope studded with thick-trunked oaks and almost no underbrush. Acorns crunched beneath their feet.

"Sometimes I eat acorns," Elly said. "Like the turkeys and squirrels."

"Don't acorns make you sick?"

"Not if you just eat one. They're kind of bitter though."

"The woods are different on this side," Stuey said. "The trees are bigger."

"I know. That's why my side is better."

"My side has the fairy circle."

"Do you ever see them? The fairies?"

"No, but you can tell they're there."

"What about the bears? I heard there are lots of bears over there."

"I've never seen any bears."

"You don't see them. They just jump out at you. But don't worry—as long as you're with me you're safe."

Stuey didn't believe her about the bears, but he pretended he did. With Elly Rose, pretending was fun.

"Do you come out here a lot?" he asked.

"I told you. I'm the Queen of the Wood."

"Well, on the other side, I'm King of the Wood."

"No you're not," Elly said with utter conviction. "You are my Knight of the Wood." She picked up a stick and tapped him on the shoulder. "I so dub thee."

They walked across the slope and soon came to the edge of a ravine about twenty feet across and ten feet deep. The bottom was a tumble of mossy rocks and broken branches. From the overhanging limb of an oak hung a grapevine as thick as Stuey's wrist. The end of the vine dangled over the center of the ravine.

"That's my swing," Elly said. "You have to go get it and bring it up here."

"Me? Why?"

"Because you are my knight-in-waiting."

Stuey had never heard of a knight-in-waiting, but he climbed down into the ravine, grabbed the end of the vine, and dragged it up to the lip.

"Thank you, noble sir," said Elly, taking the vine.

Stuey looked up the vine to the limb where it was attached. "Are you sure it's safe?"

"It's an unbreakable magic vine. Watch." She gripped the vine, took a few steps back, ran forward, and threw herself off the edge of the ravine. She swung down, her feet almost touching the bottom, then up the far side to land lightly with such grace that Stuey could almost believe the magic was real and she really was Queen of the Wood.

"Here I come!" she yelled, and swung back across the abyss. She handed the vine to Stuey. "Your turn."

Stuey gripped the vine in both hands, backed up as far as it would let him, ran at the ravine, and leaped.

There was a moment of lightness and freedom, the vine went taut — then tore loose.

Bright-green mossy rocks rushed up at him.

The first thing Stuey saw when he came to was Mr. Frankel's bristly chin, and beyond that the tops of trees, and his ears were filled with the sound of adults talking excitedly. They were moving. He was being carried through the woods, and everything hurt.

The doctor told him he had a concussion. Stuey had heard of concussions. It was when your brain got rattled around in your head.

"A *mild* concussion," the doctor said as he shone a light in Stuey's eye. "You're lucky you didn't break your skull."

"It feels like I did," Stuey said. His head was throbbing.

"I'm not surprised," said the doctor. "That's quite a bump you have."

Stuey reached up and gingerly touched the lump on his head. His mom was leaning forward in her chair with an anxious expression.

The doctor held up three fingers. "How many fingers am I holding up?"

"Twelve," Stuey said.

The doctor chuckled.

"Just three," Stuey said. "But they're a little blurry."

The doctor looked at Stuey's mom. "He'll be fine, but he'll have to take it easy for a while." He looked at Stuey. "Do you think you can do that?"

"I guess."

"That means no TV, no computer, no reading—"

"No reading?" Stuey's mom said.

"Total brain rest," said the doctor. "Keep him inside and quiet as much as possible. No loud music, no games, no visitors."

"For how long?"

"Just for the next few days. He might sleep a lot. Sleep is good. Other than the bump on the head, he has a sprained wrist and numerous contusions. He's a very lucky boy."

Stuey did not feel lucky. But he did feel tired, as if he was about to doze off right there in the emergency room. They put his wrist in a purple plastic splint with Velcro straps. He fell asleep in the car on the way home.

the compass

The day after he cracked his head, Stuey was resting his brain in bed and having the most boring birthday of his entire life. His mom had bought him a set of *Nature* DVDs—Stuey loved animal shows—but she wouldn't let him watch them. The doctor had said no TV, no reading, no anything. The boredom cure.

He was lying on his back staring at the cracks in the ceiling when the doorbell rang. He heard his mom answer it, then voices, then footsteps.

"Just five minutes," his mother said. "He's really not supposed to have visitors."

A moment later Elly Rose was standing next to his bed, peering down at him.

"You look the same," she said.

"You can't see a concussion," Stuey informed her. The bump on his head had gone down. "But I have this." He showed her his plastic splint. "I sprained my wrist."

"Well, at least you got something," she said.

"Did you come through the woods to get here?"

"I rode my bike. It's two miles."

"Your parents let you ride that far?"

"My mom says I'm a free-range kid. I get to go wherever I want as long as I wear my helmet and tell her where I'm going. Only I didn't tell her I was coming here because she'd say it's too far."

"What's the farthest you ever went?"

Elly thought for a moment. "This is the farthest. You live in a weird neighborhood. There's hardly any houses over here. Are there any other kids?"

"Not really. Just Teresa Kimball and the Charleston twins."

"You don't have any friends here?"

"I used to be friends with Jack Kopishke, but he moved. I have friends at school, but they don't live around here so I don't see them much in the summer."

Elly nodded seriously. "Me too. I mean, we just moved here so I don't really know anybody yet. Except you and Jenny Garner. Jenny's my friend who lives on my block. But you're my soul mate. Anyway, I came to say I'm sorry you got hurt." She took a breath and said, "It was dangerous and irresponsible of me to make you swing on the vine, and I apologize profusely for my negligence."

Stuey stared at her, surprised by all the big words coming out of her mouth.

"My dad told me to say that part," Elly said.

"That's okay. I'm sorry I broke your swing. I guess the magic didn't work so good."

"You must have different magic," Elly said.

I have magic? Stuey thought. He remembered the deadfall, and the voices. Was that his magic?

"I brought you a get-well present." She handed him a metal-and-glass disk with a needle in the middle, like a watch with one hand. The needle wiggled when he moved it.

"It's a compass," Elly said. "So you always know where I am. My house is straight east of here. With a compass you can always find me."

"Is it magic?"

"It might be a magical cure for concussions. It used to be my grandpa's, I think. Anyway, I found it in some of his stuff. It's really old. You can put a string through the hole and wear it."

"Thank you." Stuey hoped the magic compass worked better than her magic vine.

"It's also a birthday present."

Stuey had forgotten it was her birthday too.

"I didn't get you anything," he said.

"That's okay. You can owe me."

Stuey's mom poked her head in the door. "Time to go, Elly. Stuey has to rest now."

Some time later, Stuey's mom brought him a glass of apple juice.

"How are you feeling?" she asked.

"Pretty good. Mom, what's a soul mate?"

"A soul mate is like a close friend, someone who completely understands you."

"Like a best friend?"

"Yes, but more like someone who makes you whole. Like two pieces of a puzzle that fit together perfectly."

"Can soul mates have secrets?"

She laughed. "Everybody has secrets, Stuey. But don't think about it too hard—you're supposed to be resting your brain. Why don't you try to get some sleep?"

After she left, Stuey got out of bed and took a shoelace from some sneakers that didn't fit him anymore. He strung the lace through the hole in the compass and put it around his neck and went back to bed, the compass needle quivering just above his heart.

He drifted into something like sleep, but not sleep. Eyes closed, he felt himself floating, the same way he had felt when he was lying on the stone slab, only now he felt his new best friend's small, warm hand on his chest.

the crossing

On the second day of Stuey's brain rest, he wasn't as sleepy. His mom let him read a comic book. On the third day, she let him watch one of the *Nature* DVDs. It was about foxes. On the fourth day, he went outside and helped his mom pick beetles off her rose bushes. On the sixth day, she took him back to the doctor.

"How many fingers am I holding up?" the doctor asked.

"Three."

"Exactly right." The doctor looked in Stuey's eyes, examined the tender spot where he'd hit his head, and checked his wrist. "The swelling is down. How does it feel?"

"Good."

"Let's leave this brace on your wrist for a couple more days. Other than that, you're good to go."

"I'm unconcussed?"

"I don't remember that term from medical school, but yes, you are unconcussed, or nearly so. TV, reading, light exercise—that's all fine. But take it easy, okay? No more Tarzan stunts. And be sure to wear a helmet when you ride your bike."

The next day, without telling his mother, Stuey set off into the woods with his new compass and his backpack to visit Elly Rose. Elly would be impressed that he had walked all the way through the woods. He had a birthday present for her—a picture of a fox that he drew on his mom's good sketchbook paper. He knew Elly liked foxes, and it was one of his best pictures.

Stuey followed the compass east. Usually he stayed on the deer trails, but the compass took him through unfamiliar areas. He pushed through buckthorn and nettles, stopping every few minutes to check his bearings. At one point—he was about halfway across the woods—he looked up from his compass and found himself facing the deadfall.

The tree trunks seemed to have rearranged themselves slightly. He circled the deadfall until he found the opening. He took off his backpack and crawled inside.

Everything was the same, except for a pile of acorns in the smallest nook. Probably a squirrel's cache. He stood on the stone slab and looked at his compass. The slab was pointing east and west. He grabbed the lever branch and pushed it up. Nothing happened. He closed his eyes and tried again.

The deadfall creaked and moaned, and he felt his stomach move, like when an elevator goes down. Startled, he let go of the lever and opened his eyes. Everything looked the same. He went back outside. Nothing had moved. It must have been his imagination.

He opened his backpack, took out an apple, and ducked back inside. He set the apple in the nook beside the acorns. A present for the squirrel. Or the ghosts.

The deadfall creaked and sighed, as if saying thank you.

"You're welcome," Stuey said. His words were absorbed by the dead branches. A moment later he heard what sounded like distant laughter, and a cough.

Back outside, Stuey checked his compass and continued on his way. The earth became spongy, and shortly he came upon a cattail-fringed pond. Dozens of blue dragonflies hovered over the still surface. He found a stick and threw it as hard as he could; it splashed down halfway across. Dragonflies scattered.

He continued around the edge of the pond, through a marshy area, stepping from hummock to hummock to avoid the many small sinkholes. Several times he sank up to his ankles and had to back up and search for a new way across.

By the time he made it to the other side of the marsh his feet were soaked and his head felt as if it was floating. Maybe he hadn't completely recovered from his concussion.

He sat down on a rotting log and drank a juice box to revive himself. Looking down at his sodden, mud-caked jeans and sneakers, he thought that maybe Elly wouldn't be so impressed after all. But he had come this far. He continued his journey. His legs felt heavy. The land rose, and he was soon at the base of the slope leading up to Elly's neighborhood. He followed the edge of a ravine up the hill until he saw the broken grapevine tangled among the boulders at the bottom. One of those rocks had tried to split open his skull.

"Stupid rock," he said.

A wave of dizziness almost sent him over the edge. Stuey backed away and continued up the hill. Minutes later he let himself through the gate into the Frankels' backyard, so tired he could barely stand. He sat down on the chaise longue to rest and closed his eyes. Just for a minute.

fox

Something was tickling his nose. Stuey pawed at it, then opened his eyes.

Elly Rose was standing over him holding a long black feather, staring at him intently.

"I summon you from dreamland with my magic raven feather," she said.

Stuey scratched his nose and lifted his head. Elly was wearing a bright-pink tank top and even brighter green shorts. The clash of colors made his eyes sizzle.

"You were talking in your sleep."

"What did I say?"

"Something about dead trees."

"Oh." He felt a little fuzzy. Maybe he *had* been sleeping.

"I looked out my window and saw you. At first I thought you were the Mushroom Man."

"Who's that?" Stuey asked.

"He's very mysterious. I call him the Mushroom Man because I saw him in the woods picking mushrooms. I hope he didn't eat them because they could be poisonous. And then I came out here and saw the purple cast on your arm so I knew it was you and not the Mushroom Man so I didn't call the police or anything."

"It's not a cast. It's a splint. I get to take it off tomorrow."

"How did you get so dirty?"

"I walked across the woods," Stuey said.

"I walk in the woods all the time but I never get all muddy. You must've gone in the swamp. Why didn't you stay on the paths? Did you see any alligators?"

"There aren't any alligators here."

"You never know. I saw a giant snapping turtle once. It was as big as a car."

"It was not."

"Well, a toy car. A really big toy car."

Stuey sat up. He felt better—not so dizzy, but still really tired—and his wrist was throbbing.

"I brought you a present." He took the fox picture from his backpack and handed it to her. "It's a fox."

Elly straightened the somewhat wrinkled sheet of paper and examined the fox.

"That's a good fox. I didn't know you could draw."

Stuey flushed with pleasure. "I'm pretty good at it," he said. "My mom's an artist. She paints pictures of birds and stuff for greeting cards."

"I know how to make French toast," Elly said.

"I went to my secret place," he said.

"The secret place you won't tell me about?"

Stuey nodded. "Sometime I'll show you."

"My secret is a place too," Elly said. "It's called the Castle Rose."

"Is it a real castle?"

Elly nodded seriously. "It's a long ways away. In an enchanted forest."

Stuey pretended to believe her.

"I'm wearing the compass you gave me." He showed her how he had tied it to the string around his neck.

"It's not a compass. It's a magic amulet," she said. "It brought you here."

"Elly Rose!" Mrs. Frankel came out of the house. She was wearing a blue dress with white and black polka dots. "What are you—oh! Is that the Becker boy?"

Stuey nodded and stood up. The blood seemed to rush out of his head; he almost fell over but caught himself.

"Why, you're covered with mud, sweetie!"

"He walked all the way here through the woods," Elly said.

"Look at him! He's pale as a ghost!" She put her hands on his shoulders and bent down and looked in his eyes. "Are you feeling all right, sugar?"

"He made me a picture of a fox," Elly said.

"I'm just sort of tired." Stuey heard his own voice as if it was coming from far away.

"I'm calling your mother."

free-range

Stuey's mom was really mad. As soon as they got in the car she launched into him.

"What on earth were you thinking! Traipsing off through the woods when you're supposed to be convalescing!"

Stuey had never heard the word *convalescing*, but he got the idea.

"The doctor said I was okay," he said.

"You scared poor Maddy Frankel half to death. You know she almost called an ambulance?"

"I'm sorry."

"Stuey . . ." His mom's voice softened. "You have to give yourself time to recover. You had a serious concussion."

"I just got kind of tired is all."

"Well, I don't want you in that woods for at least another week, you hear me?"

"Okay." He was too tired to argue.

That night after dinner, Elly Rose called.

"I wanted to make sure you're okay," she said.

"I'm okay. Except my mom's kind of mad. She says I'm still *convalescing*."

"I put the fox on my wall."

That made Stuey feel warm inside. "I can draw horses too."

"I'm getting a horse. My dad says I can't have one because we don't have room, but I'm getting one anyways. White with brown spots. I already have a name for him. Spotster."

"My mom says I have to stay home for a whole week."

"You know what you should do? You should invite me over."

"Okay."

"I can get my mom to drive me over tomorrow. She didn't like it when I rode my bike."

"I thought you were free-range."

"I am, but she says two miles is too far."

After they hung up he went to find his mom. She was in her studio working on a painting of a crow. She'd been working on the same painting for days.

"How come you're still doing the crow?" Stuey asked.

"Oh, I don't know." She set aside her brush. "I just can't seem to get the feathers right."

"Can Elly Rose come over tomorrow?"

"I suppose that would be all right. I'll call Maddy Frankel and make sure it's okay with her."

"Can I have some paper to draw on?"

"Of course." She opened a sketchpad and carefully tore out a sheet of white drawing paper. "What are you going to draw?"

"A horse with brown spots."

spotster

Elly Rose and her mother showed up the next day at noon. Stuey and his mom met them on the front walk. Elly was carrying a plate of chocolate chip cookies.

Mrs. Frankel buried her fingers in Stuey's hair and told him how much better he looked. After a bit more fussing over him, she looked around the house and told Stuey's mom how *charming* and *unusual* it was.

"It's been in my family for three generations," his mom said. "My grandfather built it."

"Really! My grandparents were originally from here! But I grew up in New York. We just moved back. I wonder if our grandparents were acquainted, back in the day."

The two women went inside, both talking at once.

Stuey said, "Is your mom going to stay?"

"Once she starts talking she kind of doesn't stop," Elly said. "You have a big house."

Stuey pointed up at the third floor. "That's my room up on top. It's the only bedroom on the third floor. Gramps's room was right under mine, the one with the shades drawn."

"Is it spooky?"

"Not really. But we have a lot of room."

"Do you want a cookie? I made them myself. Mom helped."

"Let's go to the orchard. There's a picnic table there."

"We can have a cookie picnic," Elly said. They walked around the house and back to the orchard. Elly stopped at the gravestone.

"Is it real?" she asked.

"It's my grandpa's. He's buried here."

"That's definitely spooky. We have a gravestone in our basement, but it's made out of plastic. My dad puts it out on Halloween." She looked up. "You sure have a lot of apple trees!"

"My grandpa planted them," Stuey said. "They're all different kinds of apples, only most of them get kind of wormy. We don't believe in spraying. They're organic."

"We have a cherry tree. My mom is going to make cherry pie. We have a rhubarb plant. She made rhubarb pie. It was kind of yucky."

They sat at the picnic table and ate cookies until there were only two left.

"We should save those for our moms," Elly said. She stood up and looked toward the back of the orchard. "You have a really big yard."

"It's ten acres," Stuey said. "Only part of it is grass though—if you keep going through the orchard you get into the woods."

"I'm bored," Elly said.

"Do you want to bring the cookies to our moms?"

"No. They're even boring-er."

Stuey tried to think of something not boring. He remembered the golf green in the poplars.

"You want to see the fairy circle?"

That got her attention.

He said, "I mean, I've never actually seen a fairy there, but it's kind of cool."

"Where is it?"

"In the poplar grove."

"Is it far? My mom says I'm supposed to stay here."

"That's *boring*," Stuey said with a grin.

Elly grinned back and looked toward the house. "They'll be in there talking forever."

"Let's go."

They crossed the meadow and slipped through the ring of poplars to the circle of creeping bent. Elly had a peculiar expression on her face. Stuey was afraid she was going to say it was boring, but she sank to her knees and ran her hands over the smooth green surface, then looked up at him, eyes wide with wonder.

"Do you think the fairies are watching us?" she asked.

"For sure."

"I wish I had fairies at Castle Rose but I only have elves."

"How big are elves?"

"Well, they're invisible so it's hard to say. Probably the same size as Grimpus."

"Grimpus?"

"My cat."

"Oh yeah. Your one-eyed cat that doesn't like people."

"Except for me. I think he might be part elf because sometimes he's invisible too."

"Same with the fairies. Actually, this is just what's left of an old golf green. The whole woods—everything between your house and my house—used to be a golf course. My great-grandfather built it, but then when he died my great-grandmother had to sell it."

Elly gave him a look. "You're making that up," she said.

"I'm not. It's true. And when I grow up I'm going to make a lot of money and buy the woods back again."

"How?"

"I'll be a bootlegger." He liked the way Elly was staring at him. She didn't speak for a few seconds, which was unusual. "Maybe a murderer too," he added.

"Why did your great-grandma sell the golf course?"

"It was haunted."

Elly Rose grinned and nodded. "With fairies and ogres?"

"I'm not sure about fairies and ogres," he said. "But I'm pretty sure there are ghosts."

When they got back, their moms were in the orchard standing by the picnic table.

"Where have you been!" Stuey's mom said.

"Just in the meadow," Stuey said. It was sort of true; they *had* just crossed the meadow.

His mom gave him a suspicious look. "I was afraid you'd gone off exploring."

"We saved you two cookies," Elly said.

Mrs. Frankel looked sideways at Stuey's mom and said, "I think it's time for us to leave, Elly."

"But we just *got* here!" Elly said.

"It's time to *go*." There was something weird about

the way she said it. And Stuey's mom seemed really stiff, with her arms crossed.

"Just a minute," Stuey said. "I have something for you." He ran to his room and grabbed the picture he'd made. Back outside, Elly and her mom were already in their car. Stuey handed Elly the picture through the car window.

"It's Spotster," he said.

13
the mushroom man

"This is the most boring-est boring week ever," Stuey said to Elly Rose, using her favorite word.

"What boring thing are you doing?" she asked.

"Talking to you on the phone."

"I mean except for that."

"TV, reading, games, drawing. I'm making you another picture."

"What of?"

"It's a surprise." He was drawing a picture of her cat, Grimpus. He had never seen Grimpus, but he figured one-eyed gray cats all looked pretty much the same, especially the invisible ones.

"My mom doesn't want to drive me over there

anymore, and she won't let me ride my bike. She's being weird."

"Yeah, mine too. She said your mom was dredging up *ancient history*."

"Dredging?"

"Yeah. She said sometimes when bad things happen it takes forever for people to get over it."

"So they're mad about something that happened a long time ago?"

"I guess. Which is weird because you guys just moved here. But *we're* still friends, right?"

"*Best* friends," Elly Rose said.

Saturday morning, Stuey's mom finally consented to let him go play in the woods.

"But not too far," she said. "I don't want you trekking all the way to the Frankels' again. And no swinging from vines."

"I promise," he said. All he really wanted to do was go back to the deadfall. He threw a juice box and an orange in his backpack, put the compass around his neck, and headed off through the orchard. The apples were only the size of walnuts, but he picked one anyway. If Elly Rose could eat an acorn, he could eat a green apple. He gnawed on the bitter, sour flesh as he crossed the meadow.

The tall grasses were sagging with dew; by the time

he reached the poplars his jeans were soaked from the knees down, but he didn't mind. As he approached the oak knoll he tried to be as quiet as possible. He had once seen a flock of wild turkeys there eating acorns. Halfway up the hill he stopped and listened for their distinctive soft clucks.

Instead he heard someone humming.

Stuey remained perfectly still. He couldn't tell what the song was, and maybe it wasn't really a song at all. It sounded like *da-dee-dah-dah, dah-dee-dah* over and over again. Stuey crept forward until he could see the top of the hill. At first he saw nothing but trees—then one of them moved.

It wasn't a tree. It was a man. A man with a neatly trimmed beard, wearing camouflage that looked like tree bark.

Stuey crouched behind a log. The man was walking slowly in a circle, humming his little tune. He stopped and bent over. Stuey saw the flash of a knife blade. The man cut something on the ground, put it in a cloth bag hanging from his shoulder, and continued circling. *Da-dee-dah-dah* . . . A few steps later he stopped and bent over again. He held up his prize. This time Stuey could see it clearly—a bright-yellow mushroom.

The Mushroom Man! Stuey's heart was pounding so hard he was afraid the man would hear it. Looking down, he saw several of the yellow mushrooms on the ground next to him. The Mushroom Man would be coming his way soon.

Slowly, as quietly as possible, he crawled backward down the hill until the Mushroom Man was out of sight. He wanted to run home and call Elly to tell her what he'd seen. But he also wanted to go to the deadfall, because that was what he'd set out to do. He could call Elly later.

He took out his compass. He could head northeast from the cedars, then angle south once he was safely past the Mushroom Man. It was an unfamiliar route, but he was pretty sure he'd be able to find the deadfall eventually.

It took longer than he expected. He had to retrace his steps a few times to avoid a patch of nettles and a shoe-sucking bog, and got so tangled in a buckthorn grove he thought he'd never get out. And then he had to run to escape a cloud of biting gnats. Finally—scratched, sweaty, muddy, itchy, and exhausted—he saw a familiar crown of dead branches.

He took off his pack and dragged it with him into the cool, quiet interior.

"Welcome."

Stuey's heart stopped. He looked toward the sound of the voice, at a small figure tucked into the smallest nook.

"Welcome, brave knight, to Castle Rose."

ancient history

"How did you find me?" Elly wriggled out of her nook.

Stuey was speechless.

Elly jumped up on the slab and spread her arms. "I *told* you I had a castle! This is where my throne will go. And my dragon will perch on the roof. You're the first person ever to find it. I must've summoned you here with my magic."

Stuey said, "I . . ."

"Speak, brave knight! Your queen commands!"

Stuey said, "This is *my* secret place."

Elly tipped her head. "Yours?"

He nodded.

"No," she said with utter certainty. "This is Castle Rose."

"Well, *I* was here first."

"No you weren't."

They stared at each other, neither of them speaking for what felt like a long time. Finally, Elly Rose sat down on the edge of the slab.

"So we have the same secret place?" she said. "No more secrets?"

"I guess—except this isn't a castle. It's more like a . . . like a ship. I mean, it *moves.*"

"Moves where?"

"I don't know. It always comes back to the same place. And sometimes I hear stuff, like music and voices."

"Me too." Elly nodded several times. "Voices arguing, but they don't make any sense. It's kind of spooky."

Stuey sat down next to her. "You know what? Maybe it's a ship *and* a castle. A castle that moves!"

"I read a book about that. I read lots of books. I read one about a girl who travels through time, and a book about a girl that lives in a cave, and one about a little dog that turns into a wolf."

"My grandpa wrote a book," Stuey said. "It's called the *Book of Secrets*. Nobody has ever read it."

"If somebody read it, it wouldn't be a book of secrets anymore."

"I mostly like books with pictures. I like to draw."

"We can hang pictures here. It'll be like our own

secret moving castle, with pictures. This can be our meeting place while our moms are mad at each other."

"I don't get how come they're mad."

"I asked my mom. She said some people don't like Jews."

Stuey was confused. "But . . . we're not Jewish," he said.

"*We're* Jewish, silly."

"Oh." Stuey had no feelings one way or the other about Jews, and as far as he knew, neither did his mom. It was just another religion, like Catholics and Lutherans, except instead of Christmas the Jews had Hanukkah. "I don't get it."

"She said the golf course wouldn't let Jewish people join, and that it was your family's fault."

"But you guys didn't even live here then!"

"My mom's grandpa and his brother did, but my mom's parents moved to New York. Last year my mom's uncle died and left us his house. That's why we moved back here. Then, when my mom was talking to your mom, she found out that your family had owned the golf course. My dad thinks she's being silly, but that just makes her madder. Grown-ups like to argue about stuff."

"Like the preservation society. At least my mom and your dad are on the same side."

"Yeah. My mom thinks the woods are dangerous, but my dad says it's okay to play out here if I don't go too far."

"I saw the Mushroom Man," Stuey said.

Elly's eyes went wide. "Was he humming?"

"Yes!"

"I've seen him twice."

"Did he see you?"

"One time, I think. But I ran away before he could get me."

"Did he chase you?"

"I don't know. I didn't look back. And I didn't tell my mom because if she knew about the Mushroom Man she wouldn't let me out of the house."

"I'm pretty sure he didn't see me."

"That's good. He has a knife, you know."

When Stuey got home he found his mom in her studio staring at the same half-finished crow painting she'd been working on for a week.

"Mom, does our family hate Jewish people?"

Stuey's mom lowered her paintbrush and gave him a careful look.

"Of course not! Why would you ask me that, honey?"

"Elly Frankel says that's why her mom is mad at us."

"You talked to Elly?"

"On the phone." Stuey was surprised when the lie popped out of his mouth. He was afraid that she wouldn't like him and Elly meeting in the woods.

"I see." She sighed, rinsed the brush in a jar of water, wiped her hands on a rag, and turned on her stool to face him.

"Stuey, do you remember when Grandpa Zach was talking about his father? About how he built the golf course and how he was being prosecuted by a man named Robert Rosen?"

"Because he was a bootlegger," Stuey said.

"Among other things. I never knew your great-grandfather—he was gone long before I was born—but I know some things about him that Grandpa Zach didn't tell you."

"Like what?"

She pursed her lips, as if carefully considering what she was about to say. Stuey started to get scared. He wasn't sure he wanted to hear it.

"Grandpa Zach always wanted to believe the best about his father, but the truth is, your great-grandpa Ford cut a lot of corners."

"What does that mean?"

"He wasn't just a bootlegger, honey. Even after he gave up smuggling, Grandpa Ford still did business with his gangster friends. A lot of the equipment he used to build the golf course had been stolen, and he ran an illegal gambling operation out of the clubhouse. He bribed the police and politicians to overlook his crimes, but Robert Rosen, the district attorney, was determined to put him in prison.

"One time Rosen tried to serve him papers demanding that he testify in court. Grandpa Ford punched him in the face, grabbed the papers, and tore them up. Even the police he'd bribed couldn't overlook that—Grandpa Ford spent a week in jail before his lawyers got him out. He was furious—so angry he called Rosen and threatened his family. Or so Rosen claimed."

"If all that happened before you were born, how do you know it?"

"From my grandmother. Grandma Ford was a tough old lady, and she liked to tell stories about the olden days. When I was a girl, I thought it all very romantic, very Wild West. Of course, when my mother found out Grandma Ford was telling me about our family's criminal past, she put a stop to it."

"Like you didn't want Gramps telling me about the bootlegging."

"Well, yes, I suppose."

"So how come you're telling me now?"

"You asked me about Elly's mom being mad at our family. The reason is that when Grandpa Ford opened the country club back in 1937, he thought that the club should be just for Christians. Jews weren't welcome."

"Why?"

"Prejudice, bigotry, racism, fear, ignorance . . . I don't know." She shrugged. "It was the way things were back then. People of color weren't welcome either—unless they were groundskeepers or caddies. The wealthy, white, Christian people who joined the country club felt that by excluding others they could make themselves more . . . special."

"That's stupid."

"Yes, it is. We've become a better people, in some ways. At least I hope so, but we have a long ways to go. Even today there are people who say bad things about Jews, Muslims, people of different races—anyone who isn't like them. I like to think that Grandpa Ford never actually *hated* anybody for being Jewish. I think it was just a business decision for him. A very unjust decision. There were several Jewish families in Westdale, and a lot of bitterness over the club policy. Who could blame them? Especially after World War II, when millions of Jews were slaughtered by the Nazis. The district attorney, Robert Rosen, was Jewish. I suspect that he would not have been so intent on prosecuting Grandpa Ford otherwise."

"He was mad because he couldn't join the club?"

"I think it went beyond that. The two men were so

different. Grandpa Ford was an uneducated man who grew up poor and had to fight and steal to build his fortune. He saw Robert Rosen as a privileged, self-righteous know-it-all. And Rosen thought Grandpa Ford was a good-for-nothing crook.

"When the two of them disappeared, things got even worse. Mrs. Rosen was sure Grandpa Ford had killed her husband. Your great-grandmother claimed the opposite, even though there was no proof that either man was dead. Grandma Ford took over the club after Grandpa Ford disappeared, but she didn't change the policy—Jews were still not welcome at Westdale Country Club. The matter wasn't resolved until the golf course closed two years later and Mrs. Rosen moved away."

"But that was so long ago. Why is Mrs. Frankel mad at *us*?"

His mom's shoulders slumped. "When Daddy died, I thought this would all go away. That family history he was writing . . . maybe it was a good thing he never finished it . . . but he was right. The past *doesn't* go away. It lives on in people's hearts. We all pay a price for the sins of our ancestors."

Stuey was confused. He didn't get what that had to do with anything.

His mom put her palm on his cheek and looked at him sadly.

"I suppose you'll find this out sooner or later, so I may as well tell you. Maddy Frankel's maiden name was Rosen."

Stuey still didn't get it.

His mom compressed her lips, then said, "Robert Rosen was Elly Rose's great-grandfather."

cherry pie

Every chance he got, Stuey went to the deadfall. Sometimes Elly was there and sometimes she wasn't. He gave her the picture he'd made of Grimpus—a gray cat with one yellow eye and one eye covered with a black patch. Elly looked at it for a long time without speaking.

"Do you like it?" he finally asked.

"It doesn't actually look like Grimpus," she said.

"Oh. Sorry."

"It's more like what Grimpus would look like if he was a pirate." She grinned. "I love it. Grimpus will love it too." She tucked the drawing carefully into her bag. "You're a really good artist."

Stuey never told his mom that he was meeting Elly, and Elly kept it secret from her parents. At Castle Rose, they were in their own secret world.

"What on earth do you do in those woods?" his mother asked one day as he was putting on his backpack.

"Nothing. Just explore. I saw a weasel once. Sometimes I see turkeys."

"I used to go out there when I was a girl," she said. "It wasn't so much of a woods back then—the trees were smaller. There weren't so many animals. You could still see the old fairways. But Daddy didn't like me playing out there."

"Because of what happened to his father?"

"I suppose." She smiled, her eyes losing focus as she looked into the past. "I miss Grandpa Zach."

"Me too."

"This house seems so big now. Sometimes I think it's too much for just the two of us. The orchard is overgrown, the house needs paint, and I just don't have the time."

Stuey thought about all the hours she spent lying on the old sofa in her studio, staring up at the ceiling.

"I can help more," Stuey said.

"Honey, you're a huge help just by being here." She put her hands on each side of his face and smiled sadly. "I don't know how I'd go on without you."

"I could mow the orchard."

She shook her head. "I don't think you're old enough to operate the mower," she said. "But I'll tell you what you can do."

She went back to her studio and returned with a small camera. "Here." She showed him how it worked. "If you see that weasel again, you can take a picture. Or any other animals you see. Maybe I can use them for my paintings."

As he made his way into the woods, Stuey felt as if the trees were closing ranks behind him, as if he was leaving behind the unpainted house and the overgrown orchard and his mom's sadness, entering another reality. At the Castle Rose, everything was possible.

On the way there he took pictures for his mom: a jack-in-the-pulpit, a cone-shaped snail, and a spiderweb beaded with dew. At the hollow log where he had seen the weasel he stopped and waited quietly for a few minutes, but the weasel did not appear. Stuey wasn't surprised—in the woods, things only show up when you don't expect them. Every time he went out he expected to run into the Mushroom Man, but he had only seen him that one time.

The grasses around the deadfall were trampled from his and Elly's many visits. He knew she wasn't there—he could always tell. Maybe she would show up later.

Getting in and out of the deadfall was easier now—he had enlarged the opening by breaking off a couple of small branches. Inside, Elly had tied some of his pictures to the walls with colored ribbons. The smaller nook—Elly called it their cupboard—now held two plastic mugs with matching plates, a bottle of water, and several juice boxes. They had swept up the scattering of leaves and other forest material. Underneath was a layer of hard-packed white sand.

Stuey remembered what Gramps had told him—that the old golf course had twenty-seven greens. He went outside and walked around the deadfall, kicking aside leaves. After a few minutes he found it. A patch of green, about the size of a manhole cover. It looked like moss, but when he knelt down and ran his hand over it he could tell it wasn't. It was *creepy bent*—a little bit of golf green that had survived.

Gramps stood here, he thought. *Right here, on this spot.* And so had his great-grandfather the bootlegger.

"What are you doing?"

Stuey jumped up, his heart pounding. Elly was standing behind him.

"I didn't hear you," he said.

"I came under a spell of silence. What were you looking at?"

"Fairy grass," he said, pointing. "I bet this used to be a golf green."

Elly took off her backpack and bent over to examine the patch of green. "The fairies here must be extra small."

Stuey wanted to tell her how his grandpa and his great-grandpa had been here many times, right where they were standing. He hadn't said anything about what his mom had told him. He was afraid if she knew how much their great-grandfathers had hated each other, she might hate him too. But he could feel it building up inside him, the pressure of a secret wanting to get out. That was how secrets were — the longer and harder you held them in, the more they wanted to get out.

Elly stood up and said, "My mom has her book club. I'm supposed to be over at Jenny's. I don't have to be home for a couple hours." She lifted her backpack. "I brought pie."

Stuey followed her into the Castle Rose.

"My mom made it from our cherry tree." She pulled out a paper bag stained with cherry juice. "It got kind of squashed." She transferred the slices of slightly squished pie onto two paper plates and handed him one. "I forgot to bring forks."

"That's okay." They sat down on the slab facing each other. Elly's lips twitched into a smile; a coil of hair fell from behind her left ear onto her cheek. Her dark eyes glittered in the half light.

What went on inside her head? They'd spent hours and hours talking about everything, but Stuey still couldn't figure her out. In a way it was like they were from different planets, and this was a magical place where they could be together.

He forced himself to look away so she wouldn't think he was staring at her.

"What?" she said.

"Nothing."

"You were looking at me weird."

"I was just thinking about aliens," he said.

"You think I look like an alien?"

"No! I mean, I think we're both aliens. I'm from a planet where everybody is blond and chunky and we don't talk much. I think you might be from Planet Opposite."

"Because I'm skinny and have curly hair and I talk a lot?"

"And your mom makes pie. My mom never makes pie. She's like, *Eat your brown rice!*"

"Does she make you eat kale?"

"Sometimes."

"I think I like my planet better," Elly said. She picked up her slice of pie in both hands and took a small bite. Cherry filling squirted onto the corner of her mouth. She laughed and licked it off. Her tongue was like a cat tongue—long and pink and pointed. Stuey's tongue was blunt and pale. She was fast, he was slow. His fingers were short and thick, hers were long and nimble. If Elly Rose was an elf, he was a troll.

She was waiting for him to taste the pie. He picked up his slice and took a bite. The cherry filling was achingly tart and astonishingly sweet. The buttery crust crumbled and melted in his mouth. Stuey closed his eyes, overwhelmed by the dizzying textures and tastes and smells. He swallowed, opened his eyes, and said, "Wow."

"You like it?" Elly said.

"It's the best thing *ever*." He ate the rest of the slice in three huge bites—he couldn't stop himself. Elly watched him, grinning.

"On your planet, people eat really fast," she said. "If you ever invade us you'll hog all our pie."

"Only if it's cherry."

"On my planet all the pies are cherry."

Stuey watched her finish her pie.

"I don't really think that," he said.

"Think what?"

"That you and I are that different. We have the same birthday."

"We both like pie," Elly said.

"Our moms are both weird."

"We have Castle Rose."

A sound from outside caught his attention.

"Shhh!" Stuey went to one of the openings and looked outside. "He's here," he whispered. The Mushroom Man was standing about twenty feet away, looking at something on the ground, humming *da-dee-dah-dah, dah-dee-dah*. Stuey took his mom's camera from his pocket and aimed it through the crack. He pressed the button.

Click.

The sound of the shutter seemed terribly loud—the Mushroom Man stopped humming and looked toward the deadfall. He smiled, showing a mouthful of startlingly white teeth, then turned away and walked off through the woods.

"That was a close one," Elly whispered. "He almost got us!"

"I think he heard the camera."

"I'm glad he's gone."

"Maybe he's a ghost," Stuey said.

Elly's eyes widened. "Really?"

Stuey liked when she looked at him that way, as if

he was the only real thing in the universe. "Sure. My grandpa used to say there were ghosts here."

"Did he ever see any?"

"He said he did." Stuey felt something inside him give way. He couldn't hold it in. No more secrets. "One of them might be my great-grandfather. Or yours."

Elly tipped her head, giving him a quizzical look.

"It's *ancient history*," Stuey said, quoting his mom. His voice sounded strange. "But I think it might be why your mom is mad at my mom." He sat down on one end of the slab. His heart was pounding. Elly sat across from him and waited silently for him to continue.

Stuey took a deep breath and looked down at his stubby-fingered hands. The stone beneath him felt as if it was sinking and turning, a sense of moving without actually going anywhere.

"Do you feel that?" he asked.

Elly nodded, eyes wide, hands flat against the slab, bracing herself.

Stuey told her the story of how his great-grandfather was a bootlegger, and how the district attorney had tried to catch him and failed.

"The district attorney was your mom's grandpa," he said, looking up at her. Elly was staring at him, swaying slightly. She looked small. She looked scared.

"My mom told me my great-grandfather was killed by a gangster," she said in a tiny voice.

Stuey shook his head and looked down at his hands. "My great-grandfather wasn't a gangster. He was a bootlegger." He told her about how Robert Rosen kept chasing after Stuart Ford even after he quit bootlegging, and how the two men had hated each other, and how one evening they met on the golf course and were never seen again.

It was the longest he had ever talked without Elly Rose interrupting him. He looked up at her again. His eyes wouldn't quite focus. He blinked. Her image seemed to waver, as if seen through water. He wiped his eyes, but the blurriness did not go away. He looked back at his hands. He could see every detail, every crease, the fine blond hairs on the backs of his fingers, the dirt beneath his nails, the smears of cherry pie filling.

"Did your great-grandpa kill mine?" Elly's voice sounded as if it was coming from the bottom of a well.

"No!" He kept looking at his hands. "I mean, nobody knows what happened. Grandpa Zach said he thought they hated each other so bad they just sort of hated each other right out of existence."

Elly didn't say anything—all he could hear was the sound of his own breathing.

"It was a long time ago," he said.

Elly's eyes were huge and her mouth was open and she was clutching her hands over her chest. Her mouth was moving but he couldn't hear what she was saying. She looked weirdly pale, even her clothes.

"Elly?"

She held out her hands. As she was about to touch him, her fingers became foggy tendrils. He could see right through her, as if she had turned to mist.

"Elly?" he said.

He reached out for her, but she was gone.

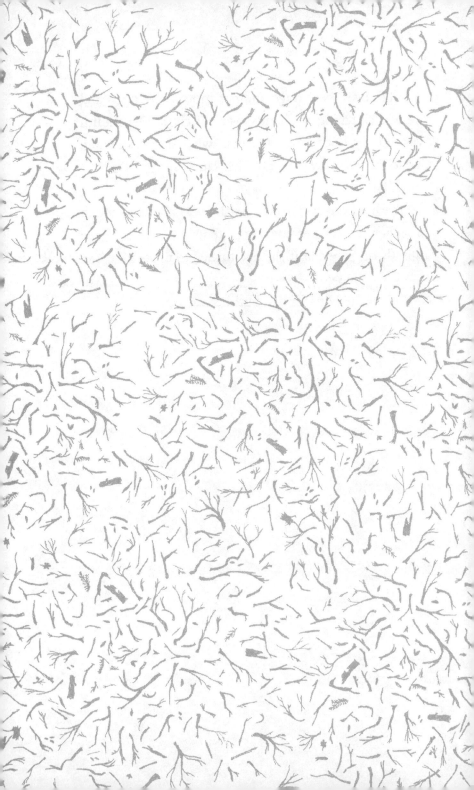

gone

detective roode

When Stuey got home his mom was in the kitchen talking on the phone.

"No, she's not here, Hiram," she said. "I haven't seen her since Maddy brought her over a few weeks ago." She looked up when Stuey came in. "Have you seen Elly Frankel, honey?"

Stuey did not know what to say, but she saw something in his face.

"Hiram, can I call you right back?" She hung up the phone, took Stuey by the arm, and sat him down at the table.

"Stuey, is there something you want to tell me?"

Stuey told her everything. He told her about the deadfall, and how it was his and Elly Rose's secret place.

"Was Elly there with you today?"

Stuey nodded.

"Is she there now?"

"I don't know. We were talking and she just disappeared. First she got fuzzy, and I was talking to her, and then I could see right through her, and then she was gone."

She gave him a long, careful look. "Stuey . . ."

"It's true, Mom. I yelled for her and looked everywhere. I ran all the way across the woods to her house but nobody was home. Then I went back to the deadfall but she wasn't there either. I thought she must have gone over to Jenny Garner's—that's where she told her mom she was—but I didn't know where Jenny lived."

His mom called the Frankels back. Half an hour later, Mr. Frankel arrived with two policemen. Stuey led them through the woods, telling them again what had happened.

At first, the policemen were nice, and acted as if they believed him. But they kept asking him the same questions over and over, and every time he told them what happened it sounded crazier. By the time they reached the deadfall the words coming from his mouth all sounded like lies.

The smaller policeman crawled inside. It was a tight fit.

"It's like some sort of playhouse in here," he yelled from inside, shining his flashlight around. "Nobody here. Bunch of weird animal drawings hanging up. Looks like somebody was eating something."

"Elly brought cherry pie," Stuey said.

"My wife made cherry pie last night," Mr. Frankel said.

"Got something here," the policeman said. He crawled out butt first and held up a camera.

"That's my mom's camera," Stuey said.

The policeman scrolled through the photos. He paused, then showed one of the images to Stuey.

"Who is this?"

Stuey looked at the picture.

"That's the Mushroom Man," he said.

Police and volunteers tromped through the underbrush, covering every square foot of the forest. Men in chest-high waders slogged through the marsh. Dogs on long leashes ranged back and forth, scaring up rabbits and other small creatures. Everyone who lived within half a mile of Westdale Wood was questioned.

The governor sent a dozen National Guard troops. They spent the next several days combing Westdale Wood, widening their search to walk the ditches, road-sides, wooded areas, and fields in the surrounding areas.

Posters with Elly Rose's picture were taped to every store window and stapled to utility poles on every block. Elly was on the front page of the newspaper and on the evening news.

The phone rang a lot—calls from reporters who wanted to talk to Stuey. His mom wouldn't let them. She wouldn't let Stuey leave the house. But she couldn't keep the police away.

The lead investigator was Detective Roode, a dour, hunch-shouldered man in a gray suit. The first time he visited, they sat down in the living room and he asked Stuey to tell him about the last time he'd seen Elly Rose.

"We were at our secret place," Stuey said. "It's like I told the other police."

"That deadfall. Yes. Did you two go there often?"

Stuey nodded.

Detective Roode looked at Stuey's mom. "Did you know about this?"

She shook her head. "He plays in the woods almost every day. I didn't know Elly Rose was out there too. The Frankels . . . well, they didn't want them playing together."

"And why was that?"

"It's nothing." She shook her head. "Nothing to do with the kids. Family history."

Detective Roode waited for her to say more, but she didn't. He jotted something in his small black notebook.

"The last time you saw Elly Rose . . . what were you doing?" he asked Stuey.

"Nothing. Just talking. I was telling her about how my mom's grandpa built the golf course that used to be here."

"Is that true?" He looked at Stuey's mom. "Stuart Ford was your grandfather?"

She nodded. The detective made another note.

"Tell me everything that happened," he said to Stuey.

Stuey told him the truth, but he had told the story too many times. The words came out flat and wooden, as if he was reading them off a script. He could tell the detective didn't believe him. He stared down at the rug as he told the last part of the story.

"Had you ever seen this 'mushroom man' before?"

"Once," Stuey said. "Elly saw him a bunch of times."

"Did either of you ever talk to him?"

Stuey shook his head.

"Do you think he might have taken Elly?"

Stuey shrugged. He had already told the detective everything.

"You don't seem very upset," Detective Roode said. "Aren't you worried about your friend?"

Stuey's mom jumped in to defend him. "He's tired. He's had to tell what happened a dozen times."

"I understand," said Roode, although it was clear he didn't understand at all.

Stuey hadn't let himself think that anything bad had happened to Elly. He hadn't let himself think at all. So much had been happening, so many questions being asked, he hadn't had time to miss her.

dana

Detective Roode brought a woman with him on his second visit. Stuey watched from his window as the two of them got out of a dark-blue sedan. A minute later his mom called him downstairs.

"Stuey, this is Ms. Johnson."

"You can call me Dana." The woman held out her hand.

Dana Johnson was a short, heavy black woman with a wide, toothy smile. Her long braided hair was gathered at the back of her neck, held in place with a complicated-looking clasp. She had on a long, rust-colored skirt and a matching jacket.

Stuey shook her hand. There were rings on most of her fingers. The gold bands on her wrist clinked.

"It's nice to meet you, Stuey," she said. "I'm sorry about your friend going missing. I imagine this has been a difficult few days."

"Kind of." He looked at Detective Roode standing behind her, then back at Dana. "You don't look like a policeman."

She laughed. "Thank you!"

Stuey was confused, but he could tell by the way she smiled that she wasn't making fun of him.

"I'm not a policeman — or a policewoman — but I do work for the county. Sometimes I help the police with cases involving young people."

Stuey liked her. He liked the small gap between her front teeth that he could see only when she smiled directly at him. He liked that she talked to him like a grown-up.

"Do you mind if Stuey and I have a little chat?" she asked Stuey's mom.

"I would like to be present."

"Of course." She turned to Detective Roode. "Would *you* mind waiting outside, detective?"

Detective Roode frowned, nodded sharply, and left them. That made Stuey like Dana even more. She could make Roode go away.

They went into the living room. Dana sat on the antique comb-back chair that he wasn't supposed to touch because it was a hundred years old and not very sturdy. His mom perched nearby on the sofa arm, ready to catch her if the chair collapsed. Oblivious of her precarious situation, Dana smiled and crossed her legs. She was wearing metallic gold sandals with high heels—the opposite of his mom's clunky clogs.

Stuey sat down on the other end of the sofa from his mom.

"So, Stuey . . ." Dana laced her fingers and rested her hands on her lap. "I hear you have a secret place."

"The Castle Rose," Stuey said. "Elly named it."

Dana smiled. "Tell me about it."

Stuey told her. He told her how he'd found it earlier that summer, and how it was his secret place he would go to, and how Elly had a secret place too, and then they found out it was the same place.

"Was that okay with you? That she shared your secret place?"

"It was just funny is all. She thought it was like a castle, and I thought it was more like a ship. We decided it could be both." He liked how carefully Dana was listening, and that she didn't take notes.

"The other day—the time you last saw her—what were you doing?"

"Just talking. I was talking mostly."

"And then what?"

As Stuey told her what happened her eyes never left his face, and she nodded every time he looked at her. He thought she believed him, even when he got to the part about Elly just fading away to mist.

"That must have surprised you," she said.

"It was kind of weird."

"Has anything like that ever happened to you before?"

"You mean has anybody disappeared?"

"Or any *thing*?"

"No," Stuey said. "Except for, like, losing a sock or something."

Dana laughed. "That happens to me all the time."

"Me too."

"What did you do after she vanished?"

"Well . . . I thought maybe I'd fallen asleep or something—that I'd dreamed it. I went to look for her. I went all the way to her house, but nobody was there. I thought she was probably at her friend Jenny's."

"We talked to Jenny. She says Elly never showed up that day."

"Elly told her mom she was going to Jenny's so she could come to Castle Rose."

"I see. Tell me more about the man you took a photo of."

"We see him in the woods sometimes. He picks mushrooms. Elly was scared of him."

"Why?"

"He had a knife."

Dana nodded, thought for a moment, then asked, "Do you have other friends, Stuey? Other kids you play with?"

"I have friends at school, but they live a long ways away. There aren't any kids my age around here, not since Jack moved to Iowa a couple years ago. Jack was my best friend."

"Is Elly Rose your new best friend?"

"She . . . I . . ." A pit opened in his stomach, and in that moment he truly knew that Elly Rose was gone, and it was his fault. He should never have told her about their great-grandfathers. He didn't understand how or why, but somehow it had driven her away, made her disappear.

Dana leaned forward, a look of concern on her face, and asked him something, but her words were a mish-mash of sound.

"We have the same birthday," he said. "We're soul mates."

ptsd

After Dana left, Stuey could not be alone. The void within pulled at his skin, threatening to turn him inside out. His bones ached; his thoughts whirled and spun into an infinitely deep, infinitely empty sinkhole.

He followed his mom around the house the rest of the day, watching dully as she cleaned the kitchen, hovering behind her as she weeded her garden, standing outside the bathroom door while she used the toilet. She didn't complain. She seemed to need to be close to him too.

That night he slept in her bed and dreamed he was in the woods, lost, running, then falling. He woke up and stared at the dark ceiling until he fell back into the same dream, always the same one, again and again.

The next morning he awoke in a haze, as if the air around him was foggy and dark. His mom kept looking at him, her brow crumpled, her mouth tight. When Dana Johnson came to talk to him again he couldn't bring himself to form words. The power of speech had left him. He could nod or shake his head, but nothing she said could coax him to respond verbally.

As Dana was leaving, he overheard her talking to his mom on the front walk. After she left, Stuey found his voice, just enough of it to ask his mom what PTSD meant.

"Post-traumatic stress disorder," she said after a moment. "Sometimes when bad things happen, our minds and bodies react in strange ways. It might take some time for you to feel . . . normal again."

Stuey nodded as if that made sense, but all he understood was that there was a knot of nothingness inside him, and now it had a name.

The Westdale police chief appeared on a local news station that night.

"At this time we have no evidence indicating where Elly Rose Frankel might be," the police chief said. "We don't know whether she wandered off on her own, or if some other factors were involved, but we are leaving no stone unturned. Our officers, with help from the

National Guard, are continuing to comb Westdale and the surrounding areas."

"We have reports of an arrest—can you tell us anything about that?" the news anchor asked.

"There have been no arrests. We interviewed a possible witness, but we do not believe he is connected to Elly Rose Frankel's disappearance."

The reporter thanked the police chief and turned to the camera. "Exclusive information acquired by *Action News* has confirmed that the person questioned by police was the so-called Mushroom Man, seen here in a photo taken shortly before Elly Rose Frankel went missing." The photo Stuey had taken appeared on the screen. "*Action News* has confirmed that the photo is of Gregory Eagen, a Westdale resident. We go now to reporter Andrea Stevens, live from the Eagen residence."

The TV showed an old farmhouse, then panned to a thin, bearded man standing at the curb by a mailbox. Stuey recognized him immediately. The Mushroom Man.

"Mr. Eagen, we understand you turned yourself in to the police this afternoon."

The Mushroom Man shook his head. "Not exactly. I saw that you were showing a photograph of me on the news, and so I went in to let them know who I was, and that I had nothing to do with that girl disappearing."

"But you were in Westdale Wood that day, were you not?"

"Quite possibly. I'm a professor of mycology at the university. I study mushrooms and other fungi. I often collect samples in Westdale Wood. I have no idea who took that photo, or when it was taken, but it could very well have been that same day."

"Why were you dressed in camouflage?"

Eagen shrugged. "I often wear hunting clothes in the woods. They're comfortable."

"Did you see Elly Rose Frankel that day?"

"No. I mean, I've seen kids playing in the woods before, but I've never so much as spoken to any of them. Look, I'm just as concerned about that child as everyone else. In fact, I've been out there with the rest of the volunteers searching. But I had nothing to do with—"

Stuey's mom clicked off the TV. "You shouldn't be watching that."

"That was the Mushroom Man," Stuey said.

His mom looked at him sharply.

"He says he didn't do anything," Stuey said.

"That may be true. I'm sure the police will find out."

Stuey stared at the blank screen.

real

One week after Elly Rose disappeared, Stuey returned to the deadfall alone. His mom would have stopped him, but she was resting in her studio and didn't see him leave.

He followed his usual path, but it didn't look the same. The underbrush was trampled, saplings were bent and broken. Westdale Wood looked as if an enormous herd of bison had charged across it. The area around the dead-fall was all footprints and mud. One of the branches had been sawed off to enlarge the opening. Everything inside was gone: the blanket, the drawings, the plastic cups.

Stuey sat on the stone slab, overwhelmed by the feeling of being alone. He wished he hadn't come. He put his hand on his chest and felt the shape of the compass. He took it out and looked at it. The needle pointed north, as always. He closed his eyes and listened. There was not a breath of wind. All was silent. He waited, listening to the sound of his own breathing. Faintly at first, as if miles away, he heard the music, and the voices. He felt the stone beneath him rise, then rotate.

He opened his eyes. The compass needle was wobbling.

"Where did you go?"

He looked up. Elly was sitting across from him, as real as anything.

He tried to say her name, but his mouth fell open and nothing came out.

"Why did you go? Where have you *been*?" She leaned toward him and stared fiercely into his eyes. "Everybody's looking for you!"

"I'm . . ." His heart was pounding and he could hardly find the air to get the words out. "I'm . . . here."

"I thought the Mushroom Man took you," Elly said. "Everybody did. Why did you go? My mom won't let me in the woods at all anymore. I had to sneak out. Did you run away? Where did you hide?"

Stuey reached out with his hand; Elly drew back.

He said, shakily, "I just . . . are . . . are you a ghost?"

"I'm not a ghost. You were gone."

"Me? I wasn't gone, you were. I saw you go. Everybody thinks you got kidnapped or something."

"You too! You were telling me those horrible things about your great-grandfather and it was making me feel all icky and I wanted you to stop but instead you just melted away and I tried to tell everybody what happened but nobody believed me."

"Me neither."

Stuey reached out again. Elly hesitated, then lifted her hand. Their fingers touched, then clasped, solid and warm and utterly real. Joy flooded the empty space inside him — Elly was back, but how? Had she ever been gone?

"Are we crazy?" she said. Her eyes were wet.

"I don't know. I mean, I don't know what happened, but we have to tell them you're okay. I have to tell my mom."

"Your mom was really upset. I saw her on the news. She was crying."

"My mom is fine," Stuey said. "Except she's worried because she thinks something bad must've happened to you."

"She went in the hospital. My dad says she had a nervous breakdown."

"What's that?"

"It's when you go crazy."

"She's not crazy! And she's not in the hospital. Come on, I'll show you. Then she'll see you're still here and everything will be okay."

Stuey stood up and pulled her toward the doorway. Elly held him back.

"I'm scared," she said.

"Me too."

"What if you're not real? What if *I'm* not real?"

"We're *both* real," Stuey said confidently. He wasn't sure he believed it, but he wanted to. "Look." He let go of her hand and lifted the compass from around his neck. The needle was still. "You gave me this so I can always find you."

He handed it to her.

Elly took the compass and pressed it to her chest, then hung it back around his neck.

"You keep it. I gave it to you. It's our connection."

"We should go. We can tell my mom, and she'll call your parents and everything will be like before."

"Okay," Elly said. She followed him out into the dappled sunlight.

"There were hundreds of people searching for you," she said, looking around the trampled ground.

"You too. Come on."

He started up the path toward home, but Elly didn't move. He glanced back at her. She was looking around frantically, turning in circles.

"Stuey?"

"I'm right here," he said. There was only about

twenty feet between them, but he was having trouble seeing her. She looked scared.

"Stuey?" Her voice sounded far away.

"Aren't you coming?" he said. She didn't seem to hear him. She was moving away, growing fainter, more transparent. The last thing he saw was her mouth silently forming his name, and then she was gone again.

Stuey ran all the way home. When he got there, red-faced and panting, his mom was standing by the front door talking to Dana Johnson.

"Stuey!" his mom said. "Where did you go? I've been calling for you."

"I was . . . running," he said between breaths.

"I can see that."

His mom was okay. Elly had said she was having a nervous breakdown, but she was fine.

"Did you forget that Dana was coming?" she asked.

"I guess so."

Dana was dressed in jeans and sneakers instead of the skirt and high-heeled sandals she had worn before.

"I've only been here a few minutes," she said. "Your mom says you're feeling better."

"I guess," Stuey said. That was the moment when he might have told them that he had seen Elly Rose, that she wasn't missing after all. But as he was about to speak he realized that they wouldn't believe him. "I'm okay," he said.

Dana tipped her head and said, "Stuey? Did something happen?"

"No," Stuey said. He could tell she didn't believe him.

"Okay then . . . what do you say we take a walk?" She gave him her gap-toothed smile. "Maybe you could show me your secret place."

not gone

Dana Johnson was not used to walking in the woods. She made her way across the uneven ground with exaggerated delicacy, as if every step presented an unknown hazard. Stuey had to stop and wait for her several times.

"Shopping malls are more my thing," she said. "I'm not much of an outdoors girl." It felt odd to hear her refer to herself as a *girl*.

"This all used to be a golf course," Stuey told her.

"That must have been a long time ago."

"It was. My great-grandfather built it. My grandpa said the woods *devoured* the golf course."

Dana stepped carefully over a fallen log. "I feel like it wants to devour me!"

"It's not far," Stuey said.

When they arrived at the deadfall, Dana looked at it for a long time before speaking.

"I can see why you liked it here," she said at last. "It has a magical feel to it, doesn't it?"

"Do you want to go inside?"

Dana peered into the dark opening. "Is it safe?"

"I've been in lots of times. It's nice."

Dana ducked her head awkwardly and entered. Stuey followed her in. He had never been inside with anybody except Elly. Dana made it feel small and crowded. She stood on the stone slab in a half crouch, as if the branches overhead were pressing down on her.

"It won't fall down on us?" she asked.

"It's solid." Stuey thumped his hand on one of the trunks. Dana flinched.

Stuey kicked at the ground with the toe of his shoe. "See the sand? I think this used to be a sand trap."

"I wonder how this big rock got here," Dana said. "It looks like it's been shaped—it's perfectly rectangular."

"I don't know."

"Is this where you were when Elly disappeared?"

"We were sitting right here, eating pie and talking. It felt like the stone was moving, and then she was gone."

"It *is* kind of . . . well . . . I can see how you could imagine things in this place!" Dana said. She ducked back outside. Stuey followed her. "How many times did you and Elly Rose come here?" she asked.

"I don't know. A bunch."

"And what did you do?"

"Mostly just talked. Elly likes to talk. She thought it was like a castle. I liked to pretend it was a ship, like it would float above the ground and go places."

"Go where?"

"I don't know. We always ended up back here."

Dana nodded slowly. "When I was a girl I'd lie in bed and try to make myself levitate. I was sure I could do it. I'd reach up and try to float high enough to touch the ceiling."

"Did you ever touch it?"

"I thought I did, once. I felt it." She shook her head sadly. "But it wasn't real."

"How do you know?"

"Because . . . gravity." She laughed. "I know that's boring—it's what happens when you grow up. You're how old? Ten?"

"Nine," Stuey said.

"That's a good age. Do you still believe in Santa Claus?"

"Yeah, right."

"But you used to?"

"Maybe when I was four."

"And that was okay, right? Nothing wrong with believing in Santa when you're little, but now you're older and the things that were real back then aren't real anymore. As we grow we—"

Stuey stopped listening because he saw something a few yards behind Dana, a sort of distortion, as if the air had thickened in one spot. The distortion took shape and solidified.

It was Elly Rose. She pointed at Stuey and said, "See? I told you! He's right there!"

". . . and sometimes it's hard to sort these things out," Dana was saying. She had not heard Elly speak.

"Who are you talking to?" Stuey asked Elly.

"My dad," Elly said.

"I'm talking to *you*," Dana said.

"I'm talking to Elly," Stuey said. He pointed at Elly. "She's standing right there."

Dana looked around, confused. "Stuey, there's nobody else here."

Elly looked up at her invisible father, then back at Stuey. "He can't see you," she said.

"Can you see Dana?"

"Dana? The lady from the police? Is she with you?"

"She's right here."

Dana frowned. "Stuey, who are you talking to?"

"Elly," Stuey said. "I can see her."

Elly's arm jerked up as if someone had grabbed her hand. "I gotta go." She was walking away, being pulled by her invisible father, looking back at him over her shoulder, dissolving—

Dana was talking. ". . . it's just the two of us here. Look at me, Stuey. When you . . ."

—and Elly was gone.

Dana kept talking. ". . . minds are amazing things. Our imagination fills the gaps in our perceptions and creates its own version of reality. Figuring out what is real isn't always possible, because our own brains are telling us stories . . ."

It sounded like gibberish. Stuey stared fiercely at the place where Elly had faded away, willing her to return.

". . . people imagine UFOs, they imagine monsters under the bed, they imagine ghosts . . ."

I saw her! He wanted to shout it in her face, but the way she was looking at him, her face all scrunched up with concern, he knew there was no way she would ever believe him.

He wasn't sure he believed himself.

Dana didn't have much to say on the walk home. Stuey could feel her eyes burning into the back of his neck. He looked back and caught her staring at him in a measuring sort of way.

When they got home, Dana and his mom sat in the living room and talked for a long time in low voices. Stuey didn't want to hear what they were saying. He sat on the porch steps, looking out at the apple orchard. The buzz of their voices merged with the faint rumble of trucks from the highway and the cicadas calling from the meadow. He couldn't make out their words, but he could imagine what they were saying.

The boy is seeing things. He thinks he's seeing ghosts. He should be put away, locked up, medicated.

Stuey left the porch and walked toward the orchard until he reached the stone marking Grandpa Zach's grave.

"I'm not crazy, Gramps," he said. It helped to hear himself say it out loud. "She was there. I touched her."

The gravestone was silent, but Stuey imagined his grandfather's voice:

You spend enough time out in those woods, you'll see them.

"See who?"

The ghosts.

"There's no such thing," Stuey said to the gravestone.

He could have sworn he smelled burning pipe tobacco.

no such thing

After Dana left that afternoon, Stuey's mom put her hand on his head and looked at him with this weird sad expression and said, "How is your head?"

"Fine," Stuey said.

"Dana said you thought you saw Elly Rose."

Stuey sensed from the way she was looking at him that his answer was important.

"I don't know." He sat down on a kitchen chair, mostly to get her hand off his head.

"You don't know?"

"I mean, I thought I did. But then there was nobody there."

"I see things sometimes," she said. She knelt down on the wooden floor in front of him so their heads were at the same level. "Out of the corner of my eye. The other day I was working in the garden and I sensed Grandpa standing there watching me, but when I turned he wasn't there. Sometimes we imagine things because we miss them so terribly."

"But what if I *did* see her?"

"You didn't, honey. Elly is gone. We might yet find her, but it's possible we won't. You can't be making up stories, no matter how much you want them to be true. Do you understand what I'm saying?"

"What if it was me?" he asked. "What if it was *me* who disappeared?"

She looked at him; her mouth grew small and her cheeks hollowed. Stuey had never seen that expression on her before. Was she mad at him? Her eyes glistened. Was she crying? She drew a shaky breath.

"Oh, Stuey," she said. "I would . . . I don't know how I would go on. Don't even say it. Don't even think it." She put her arms around him and squeezed. He could feel her heart.

"I miss her," he said.

"I know you do, sweetie. Imagine how Mr. and Mrs. Frankel must feel. You wouldn't want to be telling them that you've seen their daughter, would you? Giving them false hope?"

"I don't know."

"I think maybe you should stay out of those woods for a while."

Stuey thought about that. He thought about Elly all alone in Castle Rose, waiting for him. He thought about his mom — the one in Elly's world. The one Elly said was in the hospital. If that was true, she needed him. She needed to know he was okay.

"For how long?" he asked.

"Just for the time being. Just until . . . well, until you feel better."

"I feel fine."

"I know you think you do, but we can't always tell when things aren't right. Dana thinks you should go see a friend of hers. Her name is Dr. Missou."

"Why?"

"We think maybe she can help you deal with losing Elly."

"But—" He almost said *Elly's not gone,* then caught himself at the last second.

"Dr. Missou specializes in children who have suffered trauma. Do you remember we talked about PTSD?"

"It's that thing that makes you scared."

"I've made an appointment for you for Thursday morning."

"After, can I go in the woods?"

She said, "We'll see"—her way of saying *Probably not*.

"But *maybe*?"

She nodded the way she would nod when she didn't really mean it.

dr. missou

Dr. Missou was the opposite of Dana. She was a slim, older woman with blue-rimmed glasses, pale-blue eyes, and short, straight blond hair. Her thin lips were coated with brownish-pink lipstick. She wore a tan suit with dark-brown stripes and no jewelry other than a gold wedding band.

Their meeting—Dr. Missou called it a *session*—took place at her office at Clover Center, a strip mall on the east side of town. Stuey's mom sat in the small waiting room while Stuey followed Dr. Missou into her office. She sat on a wooden chair and crossed her bony legs. She had a pen in her hand and a notebook on her lap. Stuey took the only other seat, a soft armchair with floral upholstery. There were no windows in the room.

The only things to look at were several shelves of neatly arranged books and a few framed diplomas.

"How are you feeling today, Stuey?" she asked. Her lips looked like two writhing angleworms.

"Okay."

"Your mom says you're having kind of a hard time the past few weeks."

Stuey shrugged and looked at his shoes. The right one had a bright-green grass stain on the toe. He tried to rub it off with the sole of his other shoe.

"Would you like to talk about it?"

"I already said everything." Stuey sensed something predatory beneath Dr. Missou's exterior. Her eyes peered at him hungrily from behind her glasses, and when she smiled her worm lips separated, showing a set of small, slightly yellow teeth.

"Tell me about the last time you saw Elly Rose," she said.

"It was that day in the woods," he said.

"Which day?"

"You know. The day she disappeared."

"Yes?"

"I thought she'd gone home. But she was just gone. I don't know what happened to her."

Dr. Missou tilted her head. "Is that all? Didn't you tell the police you *saw* her disappear?"

"I don't know."

"And then you thought you saw her again a few days ago." The way she was leaning forward in her chair and peering at him made Stuey all squirmy inside. "Isn't that right?" she said.

Stuey shrugged.

Dr. Missou sat back and pressed the top of her pen against the corner of her mouth. She looked disappointed, as if she *wanted* him to be crazy.

"Do you have nightmares, Stuey?"

"Sometimes. Like I'm falling, or something is chasing me."

"Do you dream about Elly Rose?"

Stuey thought for a moment and decided he could answer that honestly.

"No."

"Do you ever get your dreams mixed up with real life?"

"Not really."

She frowned. He wasn't giving her the answers she wanted.

"What about when you went to your tree place—"

"The Castle Rose."

"Yes. When you went there with Ms. Johnson, you told her you saw Elly Rose. Isn't that right?"

She was trying to pin him down, to make him say

something so she could say he was crazy. He felt trapped. He didn't want to be there. He didn't want to answer her questions.

"Stuey? Is that true? Did you think you saw her?"

He remembered what his mom had said—that he shouldn't tell anybody about seeing Elly. That made him mad. Nobody really cared about getting Elly back, they just wanted him to stop talking about her. He felt something give way inside him, as if the wall between truth and lies had crumbled.

"I was just goofing around," he said. It felt as if somebody else was talking through his mouth.

"You didn't actually see her?"

Stuey shook his head. Dr. Missou wrote in her notebook.

"You told the police you heard music and voices," she said.

"Sometimes the wind in the trees sounds like music." That was true, but it was the lying part of him saying it.

"And the voices?"

"Sometimes wind sounds like voices too. But it's just wind."

Dr. Missou pressed her worm lips together. Stuey felt as if he had won a point.

"Do you miss your friend?"

"I just hope they find her soon."

"It's been a month." She tipped her head back so the fluorescent light bounced off her glasses and hid her eyes. "You don't seem very upset. What if she is never found? How would that make you feel?"

The question made Stuey extremely uncomfortable, but the lying part of him responded easily.

"I guess I would feel sad."

"Do you feel sad now?"

"I'm pretty sure they're going to find her."

"Why do you think that?"

Because I've seen her, Stuey wanted to say. *Because I know she's alive.*

"I just do," he said. "Is that wrong?"

"Of course not. Let's go back to the day Elly Rose disappeared. You were at your fort in the woods?"

"It's not a fort, it's a castle."

Dr. Missou made a note. "That's where you were. At the *castle?*"

Stuey nodded.

"I want you to close your eyes and go back to that day. Go back to the last moment you saw Elly Rose."

Stuey closed his eyes. He remembered sitting on the slab with Elly.

"What were you doing?" the doctor asked.

"Just talking," he said.

"What were you talking about?"

"I don't know," his lying self said. "I don't really want to talk about it," he said truthfully.

"You don't have to talk. I just want you to remember."

"Why?"

"Sometimes it helps to reimagine a traumatic event, Stuey. It's called imaginal exposure therapy. You remember an event over and over, and your emotional response to the memory becomes less . . . problematic."

"So the more you remember something, the less you remember it?"

"Not exactly. It's more like exercising to make yourself stronger. Now, close your eyes again and go back to that day . . ."

"Well?" Stuey's mom said as they drove home. "How did you like Dr. Missou?"

"I didn't like her much."

"Why not?"

"She thinks I'm crazy."

"No she doesn't! She just thinks she can help you get through this difficult time."

"I don't need help."

"We all need help, Stuey."

"Then *you* go see her. All she wants is for me to remember when Elly went away, over and over again."

"Yes, I discussed that with her. It's a special type

of therapy. She said it was the least invasive treatment option."

"I don't need treatment."

"I know you think that, honey, but when you come out of the woods and tell me you were talking with Elly . . ."

"I just made that up," Stuey said quickly. Stuey hated to lie to his mom, but his lying self didn't seem to mind. "I was just goofing around."

She gave him a skeptical side-eye glance.

"I was playing make-believe." *I'm playing make-believe right now,* he thought.

"Aren't you a little old for that?"

"I guess." *Except when I'm with Elly Rose,* he thought.

They turned into their driveway.

"So can I go in the woods now?"

"Tell you what. I want you to see Dr. Missou again, then we can discuss it."

slippery

That afternoon, while his mom was in her studio, still working on her crow painting, Stuey sneaked out. He had the woods to himself. The muddy boot prints around Castle Rose had dried hard and crisp. The search for Elly Rose had moved on.

Stuey sat on the slab and looked at his compass. The needle pointed north. He closed his eyes and listened.

Nothing.

A part of him wondered if his mom, Dr. Missou, and Dana were right. Maybe he had imagined it. Maybe his lies were the truth, and he had just been playing make-believe, and Elly was truly gone.

He looked again at the compass. The needle was quivering. He closed his eyes and listened harder. The faint hiss of air passing through leaves and branches. A low, distant rumble of traffic. The sound of his own breathing: in, out, in, out . . .

"Stuey?"

He opened his eyes.

"Elly." She was standing on the end of the slab looking down at him. He sat up. "Where have you been?"

Words tumbled out of her. "My parents still won't let me go in the woods. My mom watches me like a hawk. Actually, more like an owl with those big eyes, only she had to go to some kind of meeting and dropped me off at Jenny's but instead of going inside I came here and I'll probably get in trouble but I don't care."

"I'm not supposed to come here either."

"Nobody believes me. They think I'm *disturbed*."

"Me too."

"They made me see this scary doctor. I think she might be a witch."

"Dr. Missou?"

Elly's eyes widened. "How did you know?"

"They made me go see her too. She's a *specialist*."

"That's what my mom said. She has cold eyes."

"And creepy worm lips."

"I *know*! I don't like her. I just tell her lies."

"Like what?"

"I tell her I didn't see you disappear, and I never saw

you after. She wouldn't believe the truth anyway. Then she told me you might never come back. She told me you might be dead." She looked at him carefully. "You aren't, are you?"

"No! Maybe *you* are."

Elly shook her head. "If I were dead I'd be able to float around and stuff. You know what I think? I think the world broke in half. There's the woods where I live, and the other woods, where you are."

"That sounds like something my grandpa told me. He said the whole universe breaks apart all the time. Like, if I turn left there's another me that turns right, but I only know the universe where I turn left."

Elly leaned forward, her eyes darting around his face. "You think that's what happened? You turned left and I turned right?"

"Except we're both here now."

"We have to glue it back together," Elly said. "We have to do it right now! That's what I have to tell you—my parents are sending me away to school! In Atlanta! That's in Georgia. For the whole school year. They think if I go away then I won't care anymore about you being gone."

"But I'm *not* gone!" It wasn't fair. *Elly* was gone, not him—and now she would be even more gone.

"They say I'm *traumatized*." She spoke quickly. "But

I'm not. I just don't like it that you disappeared and they think I'm imagining things because I said I saw you but maybe if you come back they won't make me go. We have to fix it. We have to put it back together. You have to come with me. We have to show them."

"How?"

"Here, hold on to my hands really tight." She reached out. Stuey grasped her hands. They were warm and alive. She squeezed. *"Really* tight."

"Now what?"

"Close your eyes and wish."

"For what?"

"For the world to be stuck back together again."

Stuey closed his eyes and wished. After a few seconds he peeked. Elly's eyes were still shut tight, so he closed his eyes again and wished some more. He tried to imagine Elly's world where her parents were sending her away and everybody was looking for him. He imagined his face instead of hers on the posters. He imagined that the posters had never been.

What would happen if they put the world back together again? Would it be as if nothing had happened? Or would there be even more worlds, with more Ellys and Stueys wandering around looking for each other?

"I think it worked," Elly said.

Stuey opened his eyes. Elly was looking at him intently.

"How do you know?"

"I don't, but maybe it did."

They sat there holding hands for what felt like a long time.

"Now what do we do?" Stuey asked.

"We go home. Don't let go. We have to keep holding hands."

They stood up and went outside, Stuey walking backward so they could fit through the entrance without letting go. Everything looked the same.

"Do we go to your house or mine?" he asked.

"My house. So my mom can see you and I can stay in Westdale. And then we can go see your mom. They let her out of the hospital but now she never leaves the house. My mom had to bring her food."

Stuey didn't say anything. The thought of his mom being so unhappy made him feel sick inside. But if he went to see his mom in Elly's world, then what about his mom — his *real* mom — who was expecting him home for dinner?

"What's the matter?" Elly asked.

"What if I can't come back?"

"But that's where we're going! We're going back!"

"What if I go to where you are, and then both of us are gone from where I was?" He imagined his mother calling for him. "What about *my* mom?"

"She misses you. *Everybody* misses you!"

"If this doesn't work—if you disappear again—you have to check on my mom," he said. "Make sure she's okay. Promise!"

"I promise. Now come on!"

Stuey looked at her face, at her eyes so dark they were almost solid black, and suddenly he was afraid. It was all too confusing. What if she was a ghost taking him away to some sort of ghost world?

"My grandpa said that you can't tell ghosts from real people," he said.

The expression on Elly's face changed, as if he had slapped her.

"I'm realer than you are," she said. Her dark eyes glistened with tears. "I'm not the one who went away. *You* did."

"I didn't," Stuey said. "I'm right here."

"So am I!" She tried to pull him farther up the path, but Stuey wouldn't move. "Come on!"

"We have to go to my house first," he said. Her hands felt as if their palms were separated by a layer of oil.

"You're all slippery," she said, looking as scared as he felt.

Stuey squeezed her hands tighter. His fingers curled through her flesh as if it was soft clay; his fingertips pressed into his palms; he could see through her arms; her face blurred; her mouth was moving but he couldn't hear her—and she was gone. He was standing alone, his hands white-knuckled fists, his breath coming fast and shallow.

"Elly?"

No reply. He circled the deadfall and called her name. No sign of her. He went back inside and waited. Elly did not return that day. He returned the next day, and the next. His compass pointed steadily north. Elly never came.

lies

Stuey's second session with Dr. Missou started much like the first. She told him to close his eyes and remember the day Elly disappeared. This time he was ready for her. Instead of remembering what really happened, he imagined himself sitting on the slab listening to the sound of leaves in the wind, the birds, the hum of distant traffic. When he opened his eyes, Dr. Missou was frowning at him.

"I must've fell asleep that day," he told her, the lie coming easily. "I woke up and she was gone."

"I see," said Dr. Missou. Her eyes narrowed.

"All that stuff about her disappearing, I must've dreamed it."

"Okay, let's try something else. Try to remember what happened right after. The moment you realized that Elly was gone."

"I just thought she must've gone home."

Dr. Missou wrote something in her notebook.

"Close your eyes and remember what happened next," she said.

Stuey did so. He had run all the way to Elly's house and knocked on the door, but nobody was there. He'd waited awhile, then walked home.

"I went to her house but she wasn't there," he said. "I figured she was at a friend's. Then I came home."

"Again. This time I want you to remember being with Elly Rose, and then remember the last moment you saw her, and what happened after."

Stuey closed his eyes and thought about the last time he'd seen Elly. How they'd tried to glue the world back together and failed. He remembered the sudden vacuum inside him, how he couldn't seem to get enough air. He thought about the last few times he had been to the deadfall—the times he had been alone, with no sign of Elly. He imagined that she was really gone, that he had never seen her after the day she disappeared.

"Like I said. I must've fell asleep. I just made that other stuff up."

As the words passed his lips he almost believed them. It wasn't that hard. He could lie to himself as easily as he could lie to everybody else.

Stuey returned to the deadfall almost every day. The woods were recovering from the search parties. New plants were popping up on the trampled paths even as the older leaves began to lose the brilliant green of summer, as the acorns fell from the oaks.

He always brought his compass. Sometimes the needle moved, but only the tiniest bit. Sometimes he thought he could feel her, just beyond the reach of his senses, far away and very close. The woods still knew she was their queen, even if her parents had sent her to another city a thousand miles away.

Stuey saw Dr. Missou one more time. He told her about how he and Elly had played make-believe. How he knew the Castle Rose was just a pile of dead trees, and that Elly was gone, and that she might never return. While he was in Dr. Missou's office he believed what he said. He believed it when he told his mom the same things. It was as if he had split into two different people, a boy who told adults the things they wanted to hear, and the boy who knew the truth.

A week before school started, his mom told him he didn't have to see Dr. Missou anymore. "She tells me you're doing very well, Stuey," she said.

"I'm okay," Stuey said. Another lie.

atlanta

Elly's parents sent her to stay with her cousin Sarah in Atlanta.

"It's just for the school year, sweetie," her mom had told her.

"But I don't want to go!"

"Honey . . . you're not happy here, and we understand. It's a terrible thing, your friend disappearing like that. I think the break will do you good. You like your aunt Ginny and your cousin Sarah, don't you? Sarah goes to a really nice school. You'll love it."

"Why do you want to get rid of me?"

"Honey, we just think it will be best for you," her

father said. "You'll meet new friends, see new places—
and Atlanta is warm!"

"But what if Stuey comes back?"

Her parents had looked at each other and didn't say
anything. Elly felt tears gathering in her eyes; she wiped
them with her sleeve before they could spill down her
cheeks.

Her dad said, "Elly . . ."

Nobody else thought he would ever come back.

Nobody except her.

Sarah's school was the Rothman Academy, a kinder-
garten through eighth grade Jewish day school where the
girls all wore beige skirts and blue polo shirts with the
school logo on the chest. The boys wore dark pants and
red shirts. Her aunt promised to take her shopping, but
that first day Elly had to borrow Sarah's clothes, which
were a size too big. All day long she had to keep hitching
up her skirt.

Elly's parents weren't particularly religious—they
went to synagogue on holidays, but that was about it. She
didn't know how to be Jewish the way these kids were
Jewish. Even the younger kids seemed more mature,
more serious, and smarter than her. Most of them came
from conservative families. All the boys wore little round

caps called *kippas* on their heads, and many of the older boys also wore little leather boxes strapped to their foreheads. Elly had never seen that before. She asked Sarah about it.

"Seriously?" Sarah said. "You never saw tefillin before?"

"What are they?" Elly asked.

"Tefillin have verses from the Torah hidden inside. It's supposed to remind the boys to be good or something."

"It looks uncomfortable."

"They don't wear them all the time. Anyway, girls don't have to wear them."

Elly remembered Stuey talking about how they were from different planets. This felt like another galaxy.

The kids at the school all knew about Stuey. Sarah had told them all about it, but they still had a lot of questions. Elly didn't try to answer them honestly. She already felt like a weirdo. If she'd said what had really happened they'd all think she was as weird as she felt, so she just told them Stuey got kidnapped. After a few days of that they more or less lost interest in her.

Elly didn't know any Hebrew at all. They put her in a Hebrew class with first- and second-graders. That was humiliating. Here she was at a school where everybody was Jewish, and she'd never felt like such an outsider.

After the first few weeks she learned to fake it, but

every day was hard and, even worse, boring. If she had told them about the Castle Rose they would have laughed at her. So she hunkered down, kept her mouth shut, and pretended to be smarter and more mature than she was inside. It was exhausting.

Living with Sarah's family was just as hard. Her aunt Ginny was so nice that Elly felt like she had to say *thank you* about a thousand times a day, even when she didn't feel thankful at all. Her uncle Rob, who was her mom's brother, was a tall, silent scarecrow of a man who hardly seemed to notice her. And Sarah, who was the same age as Elly, treated her like her disadvantaged little sister— *soooo* nice and *soooo* patient it made Elly want to rip her hair out.

The one thing Elly's parents were right about was that the longer she was in Atlanta, the less she thought about Stuey. She knew he was still back there, in his own world, but that world felt farther away as each week passed.

By the time Passover arrived in April, she thought about him only at night, just before sleep, when she imagined that her bed was a slab of stone and her ceiling was a lattice of branches. Alone at night, she could still be the Queen of the Wood, and he was her knight-in-waiting.

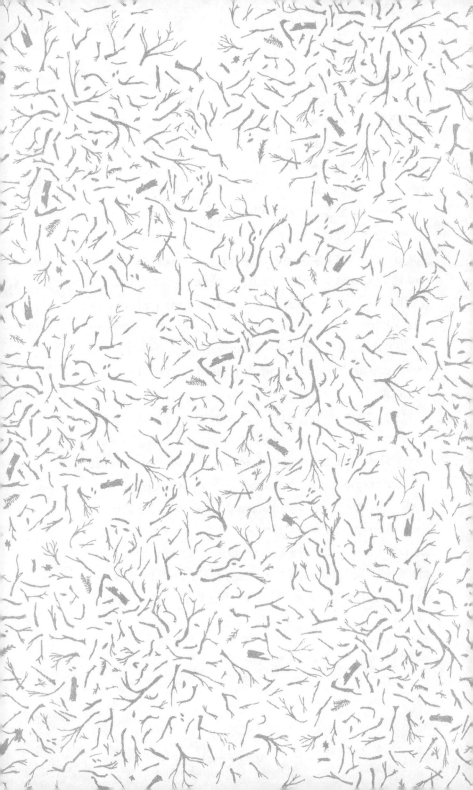

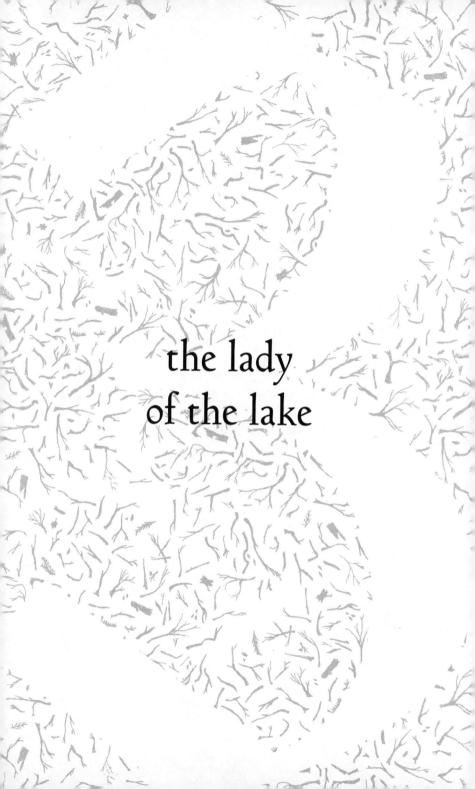

the lady
of the lake

school

Westdale had changed after Elly Rose disappeared. The main roads leading into or out of town had billboards with her face on them. Neighbors looked suspiciously at neighbors. Worried parents kept their children at home. Security cameras appeared on utility poles, garages, storefronts, and in parks.

The police bought three new squad cars with tinted windows and heavy black steel bumpers that made them look like military vehicles. Anyone from out of town was likely to be pulled over—anything from a broken taillight to driving too slowly would get them a citation. People from the surrounding communities avoided driving through Westdale.

Gregory Eagen, the so-called Mushroom Man, resigned from the college, sold his house, and moved to Saint Paul. He claimed that the Westdale police were harassing him, stopping his car for no reason and demanding to look in his trunk. His house had been searched six times. He said he couldn't walk down the street in Westdale without people giving him the "stink eye."

Elly's father quit the Westdale Preservation Society. "Westdale Wood is a hazard," he declared, reversing his previous position. "Children need a safe place to play. This unsupervised wilderness in the middle of our growing community is simply not acceptable."

Stuey's mom took over as president of the preservation society. There were petitions, lawsuits, and demonstrations. According to his mom, Forest Hills Development was giving money to the mayor and every member of city council.

"They call them 'campaign contributions,'" she sniffed. "It's nothing but bribes. Forest Hills Development—what a joke! All they do is cut down forests and level hills. Your grandfather must be spinning in his grave."

"Can you stop them?" he asked.

"I don't know, Stuey. There's an election coming up in November. We have a referendum on the ballot to make Westdale Wood a nature preserve. If that doesn't pass, the county will be under a lot of pressure to sell the land to the highest bidder." She sighed. "Sometimes I feel like we're trying to hold back the ocean tide. But we have to try."

The search for Elly continued, but it wasn't mentioned in the news as often. The posters on walls and utility poles became faded and tattered. The people of Westdale, more fearful and suspicious now, went on with their lives.

Westdale Elementary was four miles away. Every weekday morning at five minutes to eight, Stuey put on his backpack and trudged the quarter mile from his house to the bus stop on County Road 17. He waited there with the Charleston twins, who were in first grade, and the two Hawkins girls, who lived on the other side of the county road. Alicia, the younger Hawkins girl, was in Stuey's class.

Stuey was the only one who stood outside at the bus stop. The Charlestons and the Hawkinses were always driven there by their mothers. They would sit in the idling cars until the bus arrived, then pile out and follow him onto the bus.

Stuey asked Alicia about that. "You guys used to walk to the bus," he said. "Now your mom brings you. How come?"

Alicia looked at him as if he was the stupidest person on the planet.

"Because of kidnappers," she said, giving her blond hair a toss. "I can't believe your mom lets you walk."

"I haven't gotten kidnapped," Stuey pointed out.

"Well, you could be. Any of us could. The kidnapper is still out there."

Stuey wanted to say, *Nobody kidnapped Elly! She just disappeared. And she's not really gone!* But he said nothing because he knew she would never believe him.

At school that first week everybody was talking about Elly Rose even though hardly any of them knew her. Stuey was surprised by how much older and more mature the other kids were, especially the girls. He had grown too, but not that much. While he'd been playing little kid games with Elly Rose, the rest of them had done things like gone to space camp or the Grand Canyon.

Jenny Garner got a lot of attention because she was one of the few kids who knew Elly. She told everybody that Elly had been taken by the Mushroom Man.

"He probably has her locked in a basement someplace," Jenny said.

"Why would he do that?" Stuey asked.

"You are so immature," Jenny said. "You don't know anything."

Stuey wanted to say, *I know more than you! I saw her*

disappear. I saw her come back! She's not really gone! But he said nothing.

A policeman came to the school and talked to them about personal safety. To look both ways. To never be alone. What to do when approached by a stranger. When to say no. When to scream and run.

To always be afraid, Stuey thought.

the referendum

As the leaves turned yellow and orange and fell from the trees, the kids at school tired of talking about Elly Rose. It had been three months. To them, that made it practically prehistoric. Their new favorite thing to argue about was the referendum. Most of them were just repeating stuff they heard from their parents. Everybody wanted the shopping mall.

"It would be so cool," Alicia Hawkins said one day on the bus. "They want to put in a theater. We could walk to the movies!"

"But what about the woods?" Stuey asked.

"Nobody goes there," Alicia said.

"I go there," Stuey said.

"You're weird. It's all buggy. Besides, you could get kidnapped."

"But what about all the animals that live there?"

Alicia gave him that look she was so good at—the look that made him feel clumsy and stupid. "You don't know anything," she said.

People were always telling him that.

There were times when Stuey didn't think about Elly at all. When he did remember her, it felt like a soft punch to the stomach. As the weeks passed, the punch became softer. He didn't go to the deadfall much anymore, and when he went he didn't stay long. He brought his compass but no longer expected Elly to show up. When he stretched out on the slab, nothing happened—no sense of movement, only a paralyzing stillness. The voices were still there, but they sounded distant and forlorn. Without Elly the magic of Castle Rose was fading.

He thought about what his mom had said about soul mates: *They make you whole.* He hadn't really understood that until Elly went away. Without her, he was incomplete.

Twelve inches of wet snow fell on election day. The apple trees sagged. Grandpa Zach's gravestone, capped with a crown of snow, was barely visible.

The storm didn't stop people from voting. When the official results came in the next morning, they learned that the referendum to save Westdale Wood had been defeated.

Stuey was afraid his mom would be mad, but she just seemed tired. She sat in the kitchen for a long time drinking tea and paging through a photo album. Stuey sat down across from her.

"Look at this, Stuey. Do you remember?" She rotated the album and pointed to a photo. A much younger Stuey was sitting at the picnic table in the orchard, grinning over a lopsided, candle-studded cake. He was missing a front tooth. Next to him sat a dark-haired boy wearing a baseball cap.

"That's Jack Kopishke," Stuey said.

"Yes. Your seventh birthday."

Stuey hadn't thought about Jack in a long time.

"Happier days," his mom said.

It felt like a thousand years ago.

"What's going to happen now?" Stuey asked. "Are they going to wreck the woods?"

"Nothing is certain," his mom said, closing the photo album. "We've reached out to the Nature Conservancy and some other conservation groups for help, but I'm afraid it's a long shot. Everybody seems to want a new shopping mall. Do you still go to that place in the woods?"

He nodded.

"And?"

He shrugged. "I think about Elly. Sometimes I pretend she's still here."

"You miss her. We all do."

"You don't think she'll ever come back."

"It's been four months, Stuey." She held out her arms. "Come here."

Stuey went to her. She wrapped her arms around him and squeezed him and kissed his neck and said, "I can't imagine what the Frankels have gone through. I can't imagine losing you. It's been so hard. First Grandpa, then Elly Rose, and now the woods. If you were gone, I think I'd go mad. But we're still here, aren't we?"

Stuey thought about the last time he had seen Elly, how they had held hands and she had tried to take him with her. To wherever she was. He thought about how she had said his mom was going crazy.

"I'm here," he said.

stakes

Stuey made two new friends at school: Deshan Nelson, who had moved to Westdale that summer and was the only black kid in their class, and Grant Hellman, who everybody called Heck. Both Heck and Deshan liked to draw. They were impressed by Stuey's animals, especially the fox he had drawn on the cover of his notebook.

"I saw it by my house," Stuey told them. "It's a red fox."

"All foxes are red," Deshan said.

"There are gray foxes and white foxes too," Stuey informed him. "But I've never seen one."

"What about *green* foxes?" Heck asked.

"I've never heard of that," Stuey said. "But I bet I could draw one."

Deshan specialized in drawing cars with long hoods

and fire coming out of the tailpipe. Heck liked to draw faces, the uglier the better. He made a picture of Ms. Galligan with fangs, bloodshot eyes, and a wart on her nose. Ms. Galligan didn't know it was supposed to be her. She thought it was a gargoyle, and she pinned it up on the board. The three of them got the giggles so bad they had to be moved to separate corners of the room.

Stuey looked forward to school days. Deshan and Heck were fun. It wasn't like with Elly—they didn't *get* him the way she had—but Stuey liked hanging with them. At home he was snowbound. There was no place to walk to, and his mom was pretty much obsessed with saving Westdale Wood. She was always on the phone or writing e-mails.

In February she was able to enlist an organization called the Midwestern Wetland Advocates in the battle. Their idea was to turn the center of the woods into a natural wetland by putting Barnett Creek back on its original course. That would flood nearly half of the woods, forming a lake. Stuey didn't love the idea of the woods being flooded, but at least most of it would be saved. It would be better than having a shopping mall in the backyard.

The preservation society presented their new proposal to the state and county in early March. It was rejected. A few weeks later it was announced that Westdale Wood would be sold to Forest Hills Development.

That didn't stop Stuey's mom. The phone calls and letter writing continued.

"I'm going to fight this," she said. "We're going to win."

"What if we don't?" Stuey asked.

"We will," she said. "We have to. For Grandpa."

While his mother did battle with calls and letters, Stuey drew pictures, read books, watched television, listened to music, and played video games. Every now and then he would think about Elly, and it would be as if the lights dimmed for a moment. He had learned how to put her aside, in a back corner of his mind. By the time spring arrived he hardly thought of her at all.

The first day of spring break it rained, a slow, steady drizzle that promised to last all day. The last snowbanks were reduced to dirty, icy lumps. Everything looked dead and sodden and gray. Stuey had planned to go over to Deshan's house, but his mom had another preservation society meeting, so he couldn't get a ride from her.

He looked out over the dreary orchard from his bedroom window. Several of the apple trees had lost their limbs. He wondered how the deadfall looked now, after the long, snowy winter.

There was only one way to find out.

He put on his raincoat and rubber boots and trudged out into the woods.

The path was muddy and slippery; Stuey kept his hood up and his eyes on the ground. Last summer felt like the distant past, far away and blurred by time.

At the bottom of the knoll, he came upon a set of fresh boot prints. A man, by the size of them. He stopped and looked around. Gray-brown tree trunks, dead grasses, and a hazy mist of drizzle. Who would be out here at this time of year? Elly's father, still searching for her? The Mushroom Man? After a few yards, the prints veered off to the right. Stuey continued on his path, and soon a shadowy, pyramidal shape rose through the mist. The rain had darkened the cottonwood trunks nearly to black. The deadfall seemed to have sagged slightly, as if the weight of winter's snows had pressed it a few inches into the earth. Stuey peered inside. It was smaller and dimmer than he remembered. He ducked through the entrance. Elly wasn't there.

"You were never here," he said aloud. Hearing his own voice speak those words sent a hollow pang through his guts; he immediately felt horribly guilty.

"I mean, I'm not sure," he added. It didn't help. He sat down on the cold, wet slab and thought about the last time he had seen Elly. When she had tried to take him with her, to wherever she was. Had he made that up?

He felt for his compass, but it wasn't there. He had left it on his dresser. He lay back on the slab and closed his eyes. The slab moved, a small shifting, like a raft on still waters. He imagined the deadfall rising, drifting through the woods. He imagined Elly Rose sitting on the end of the slab. He listened to the faint hiss of drizzle sifting through the branches. He imagined Elly as he had seen her last, wearing a green T-shirt and jeans.

"Aren't you cold?" he whispered.

She smiled. He opened his eyes.

He was alone.

He sat up. The crinkling of his raincoat obliterated the sound of the rain. He stood up and went to the entrance and looked outside. Everything exactly the same. He ducked through the doorway and began the long walk home. He had gone only a few dozen yards when a flash of color caught his eye. A few feet off the path was a wooden stake, about three feet high, with a fluorescent-orange ribbon tied to its top.

Looking around, he saw several other stakes scattered through the woods. Earlier, with his hood up and his eyes on the path, he hadn't noticed them.

He knew what they were — survey stakes for the new shopping mall.

On the way home, he pulled up every stake he saw, even though he knew it wouldn't make any difference in the end.

stony fingers

At the end of the school year they sent Elly home. That was almost as jarring as going to Atlanta in the first place. Her mom met her at the airport in Minneapolis and covered her with perfumy kisses. She was the most dressed-up Elly had ever seen her, and she talked nonstop all the way home. As they entered Westdale, a billboard came into view with Stuey's face about twenty feet high next to giant letters spelling out MISSING CHILD. The billboard had gone up last summer. Over the winter the sun had bleached most of the color from Stuey's face, and the red letters had faded to pink. It had been almost a year since he went away.

That was how she thought about it. Stuey *went away.*

Her mom wasn't mad at Stuey's mom anymore. Instead, she felt sorry for her.

"Anne Becker is back home," she told Elly. "She was in the hospital for a time—depression, they say—but now she's back in that big house—I can't imagine how lonely it must be. Daddy and I went to see her a few weeks ago—I brought her a casserole. Noodles and cabbage. She's a vegetarian, you know; I feel so bad for her. I don't think she's eating right. She looked thin as a rail. She showed me a painting she was working on. A robin. She said the robin is a sign of spring, of hope. No mother should have to lose a child." She sighed. "Even after . . . what happened last summer . . . she still wanted to save the woods. So there's that, at least."

Elly's dad had taken over the preservation society after Stuey's mom got sick. They had finally worked out a deal between the county and a conservation group called Midwestern Wetland Advocates. Half of the woods would be saved, but the other half would be turned into a lake.

According to her dad, letting Barnett Creek go back to its original course would return the area to its "natural state"—the way it was before it had been drained to make a golf course. He showed her a map of how it would look.

The Castle Rose would be underwater. And it would

be impossible to walk from one side of the woods to the other with a lake in between. Not that she had any reason to walk all the way across the woods with Stuey gone. But what if he came back?

Everything was changing. The only thing that stayed the same was her cat, Grimpus, who was waiting for her in her room, perched on her pillow as if it was a throne.

"I'm sorry I left you for so long," Elly told him. "You wouldn't have liked Atlanta. All the cats there are mean."

Grimpus blinked his good eye. She scooped him up and hugged him to her chest.

"I'm back now, Grimpy. I'm not going anyplace."

The next morning, as soon as she could sneak out, Elly went to visit Castle Rose.

The woods had changed. A lot of the small saplings had been trampled last summer by the searchers, there were trails where there had been no trails before, and her usual path had been blocked by a fallen cottonwood. To get past the downed tree she had to detour around a boggy area, then wade through a bunch of nettles to get back to the path.

When she finally reached the deadfall, she hardly recognized it. It seemed lower, smaller, and darker—less like a castle and more like a pile of logs. Lots of new green plants had sprouted up around it. There were no tracks or any other sign that Stuey had been there.

Inside, the castle was ankle deep with blown-in leaves. She ducked through the doorway and shuffled through the leaves to the slab and carefully brushed it clean. She sat on the cool stone, feeling bereft. She closed her eyes and reached out, but felt only emptiness.

The deadfall moaned.

Elly's eyes popped open. She looked around fearfully. It must have been wood rubbing against wood, the sound of the deadfall slowly sinking into itself. She lay flat on her back and looked up at the chaos of interlocked branches above. She closed her eyes again and listened.

After a few minutes she felt as if she was floating, the same familiar feeling she remembered from before. Then came the murmuring, the sound of distant voices, and faint music. The voices slowly became louder and more strident. It sounded like men arguing, their muffled shouts garbled and distant. The stone beneath her seemed to quiver with their rage.

She opened her eyes. The voices fell silent, and suddenly she was afraid. Heart pounding, she tried to sit up, but she couldn't move. She weighed a thousand pounds. Even lifting her arm proved impossible. The slab was holding her, rough stone hands pinning her down, glittery quartz nails tearing through her shirt, digging into her ribs, dragging her into the stone.

She opened her mouth and screamed. It came out as a high-pitched squeal, but it was enough to shatter the spell. In an instant she was on her feet and out the doorway.

What had just happened? A dream? She checked herself. Her T-shirt looked fine. No rips. It had to have been a dream, but she could still feel it, and . . . voices? She could still hear a distant mutter. It sounded as if it was coming from the other side.

Elly edged around the deadfall and saw a man standing about twenty feet away. At first she thought it was the Mushroom Man, but it wasn't. This man was clean-shaven, he wore glasses, and he had on an old-fashioned suit. His slightly hunched, scarecrow-like look reminded her of her uncle Rob in Atlanta. The man was facing to the side and he had one hand in his pocket. His mouth was moving. She could hear sounds but couldn't make out his words. It sounded like the unintelligible voices she had heard inside the castle.

Maybe he's one of the detectives, she thought, *still looking for Stuey, talking on one of those wireless headset phones.*

Whoever he was talking to, the scarecrow man was angry—his face was red, and the veins on his thin neck stood out. Strangest of all, his legs were buried up to his shins, as if he had sunk into the earth.

She looked around to see if there was anybody else there. When she looked back an instant later, the man in the suit was gone.

Elly backed slowly away, her heart pounding. She turned her back on the deadfall and ran for home.

By the time Elly let herself in through the back gate, she had calmed down somewhat. She went inside. She could hear her mother down in the basement. She went up to her bedroom and changed her clothes.

It had to be a bad dream, she thought. She'd had nightmares like that before, where she was paralyzed and something terrible was coming to get her and no matter how hard she tried she couldn't move. Maybe she'd dreamed the scarecrow man in the suit too.

She curled up on her bed with Grimpus, hugging him to her chest. She had fallen asleep in the deadfall before, but Stuey had been there to protect her.

It *had* to be a dream. But did that mean that the other things that had happened—Stuey disappearing and then coming back again—had those been dreams too? She knew the difference between make-believe and the real world. She didn't really believe in elves and fairies. She knew that being Queen of the Wood was just a game—but hadn't she seen Stuey disappear before her eyes? And hadn't he come back? Hadn't they held hands and talked?

"Elly?" Her mother was standing in the doorway. "Where have you been?"

"No place." Elly sat up and gave her mom a fake smile. Her mother was real. This house was real.

"Daddy has a preservation society meeting tonight, so it will just be the two of us for dinner. I made pie."

"Cherry pie?"

"The cherries aren't ripe yet, sweetie. But it's rhubarb season."

"Oh." Rhubarb pie was *too* real.

"I'll make cherry pie for your birthday if the cherries ripen in time."

The last time she'd made cherry pie was the day Stuey went away.

"Okay."

Her mother left. Elly looked down at Grimpus, who was flopped across her lap, looking rather tired. Her birthday was in three weeks. She would be ten years old. "You're not invisible," she said to Grimpus.

Grimpus looked up at her and blinked his yellow eye.

She began to cry.

Jenny Garner had changed. She had her hair up in a sort of ponytail that sprouted from the top of her head and trickled down past her ears, and she was wearing a giant T-shirt with supertight jeans and ballet slippers. Elly thought she looked like a teenager.

Her bedroom was now decorated with posters of boy bands and handsome young actors. Her dolls were gone, except for one naked Barbie standing on her dresser.

Jenny acted different too. Sort of superior. And she wasted no time telling Elly that she had a new best friend named Shawna.

"Shawna's really cool," she said, implying that Elly was not. "Her mom does costume design at the Children's Theater in Minneapolis, so she goes to all the plays for free. We're going to see *The Wizard of Oz* next week."

"I saw that twice," Elly said.

"Not the *movie*," Jenny said. "This is a *play*, with real actors."

"Oh." Now she felt stupid. Jenny hadn't asked her anything about Atlanta, or said anything about Stuey. It was all about Jenny. She had a bunch of new clothes she had to show Elly.

"I had to wear a uniform at school," Elly told her. "We all had these blue shirts."

"Yuck! What kind of school was that?"

"A Jewish school," Elly said.

"Oh my *gawd*, that sounds like the worst thing *ever*!"

"It wasn't so bad. The kids were really smart."

"I don't know how you can stand to be Jewish."

Jenny had never said anything like that to her before. Elly felt as if she'd been punched in the stomach, and her face was getting hot. She had to change the subject before she started crying or said something awful.

"Do you ever have dreams where you can't move?"

"Sometimes in my dreams I can fly."

"I went to the Castle Rose yesterday."

Jenny gave her a blank look.

"You know. My secret place. I told you about it."

"Oh! You mean where you were when that boy was kidnapped."

"They don't know for sure if he was kidnapped."

"Or drowned in the pond or something. I would never go in those woods if you paid me a million dollars."

"They're going to make part of it into a lake, and the rest of it will be a nature center."

"I know. So stupid. I wish we were getting our own shopping mall instead. My mom says it's all your dad's fault. Hey, look at these cool boots I got on sale."

Elly did not go back to the deadfall that week. Every day she told herself she would, but the memory of that dream—it *had* to be a dream—was too vivid, too real. In her own bed, every night, she could feel cold stone fingers digging into her ribs.

birthday

Elly's mom wanted her to invite some kids over for a birthday party.

"But I don't know anybody," Elly said.

"What about Jenny?"

"I don't like Jenny anymore."

"Oh! Did something happen?"

"I just don't like her," Elly said.

"What about that girl who lives on Westwood Drive? The Johanson girl."

"She's Jenny's friend. I just want Grimpy." Elly was huddled on her bed holding her cat.

"Honey . . . oh! I know! You could invite Aimee Rosen! You like Aimee, don't you?" Aimee Rosen was Elly's second cousin. She lived all the way over in Saint Paul.

"She's only eight."

"Well, you're only nine—at least until tomorrow."

"No thank you," Elly said.

"All right, if you're sure. What kind of cake would you like?"

"I want cherry pie." Elly knew she was being difficult. The cherries on their tree were still green.

"I'll see what I can do." Her mother compressed her lips and backed out of the room.

"Mom?"

"Yes, sweetie?"

"What if I don't want to?"

"What if you don't want to what?"

"Be ten."

Her mom looked confused.

"Jenny's ten, and Jenny's mean. She threw away her dolls and all she wants is clothes and to go shopping. She thinks our whole family's stupid because Dad stopped the mall."

"Oh!" Her mom stood there blinking. "Well, I guess she's entitled to her own opinion. But turning ten doesn't have to mean you change, Elly. It's just a number."

"Then how come everybody makes such a big deal out of it? What if I don't want to grow up?"

Her mom was staring at her with shiny eyes. Elly hugged Grimpy and glared back at her.

"Oh, sugar pie, you stay just like you are forever." Was she crying? "You don't have to grow up."

"Okay then," Elly said. "I won't."

They had her birthday dinner on the patio. Her mom had made Elly's favorite: kid-size hamburgers, onion rings, potato salad, and cherry pie for dessert.

She got a lot of presents: clothes, books, and her own cell phone. She was happy to have the phone, but she had no one to call. Last year Stuey had given her a drawing of a fox. It still hung on her wall, and it was better than a cell phone.

Dad was in a good mood. He made stupid jokes all through dinner.

"When I was ten," he said, "the years were longer."

"That doesn't make any sense," Elly said.

"I know!" he said. "But it's true. The older you get, the faster time passes. Now that you're ten years old all your days will be shorter than when you were nine."

"But the years will be longer?"

"No, they'll be shorter too."

Elly thought about last summer. It seemed like a thousand years ago.

"Just think," her dad continued, "pretty soon you'll have your very own lake! Maybe for your next birthday we'll get you a kayak."

"What's a kayak?"

"It's a little boat," her mom said.

"I don't want a lake," Elly said. "I like the woods."

"There will still be plenty of woods," her dad said. "The lake will be in the middle of the preserve, with trees all around. They're going to start dredging tomorrow and taking out some of the scrub. This time next month the dam holding back the creek will be opened, and Westdale Wood will go back to the way it was a hundred years ago."

The cherry pie was too sweet and goopy. Her mom had made it with canned cherries. It was all Elly could do to choke down her slice. The cherry pie she had eaten with Stuey had been better.

That reminded her—the last time she'd seen Stuey she had promised him she would check on his mom, and she'd never had a chance to do that.

"Do you know what we should do?" she said. "We should take a piece of pie to Mrs. Becker."

"Oh, honey," her mother said, setting down her fork, "I'm sure she won't want to be bothered."

"You said she isn't eating enough. I bet she'd like your pie."

Her parents looked at each other.

"Elly, that's a nice thought, but Mrs. Becker hasn't been well the past few months—"

"That's why she needs pie! Please? Can we go over there?"

"I'm not sure it's such a good idea, honey," said her mom.

"Yes it is! It's a perfect idea! And it's my birthday so I get to do whatever I want!"

"Within reason," said her father. "We can't just go barging in on people."

"Why not? People barge all the time!"

Her parents exchanged another look.

"I think she'd really like your pie, Mom."

"What do you think?" her mom asked her dad.

"Her phone is disconnected," he said. "Last time I was there she wouldn't answer the door. But I suppose it wouldn't hurt to check on her. We can drive over as soon as we're done here."

Elly's mom nodded, then turned to Elly. "Are you sure you want to do this, honey? Anne Becker has changed . . . well, a lot."

"That's okay," Elly said. "I'll still recognize her."

pie

"Good Lord, would you look at that yard!" her dad exclaimed as they drove up the driveway. "It looks like she hasn't mowed it all year!"

"Maybe her lawn mower isn't working," said Elly's mom.

"Well if she doesn't take care of it soon the city will send a crew over to cut it, and they'll charge her for it." He stopped the car. "I suppose I could get some of the guys over to clean it up, if she'll let us."

"We could ask," Elly's mom said doubtfully.

Elly opened the door and hopped out, holding the plastic container with the pie. She ran toward the front door.

"Elly! Wait!"

She stopped and let her parents catch up. They climbed the front steps together and Elly rang the doorbell. A few seconds later she pressed it again.

"That's enough, Elly. Be patient."

Elly was patient. They stood there for almost a minute, which felt like a very long time. Finally, Elly heard a faint *clunk-ka-clunk* coming from inside. The door opened.

Mrs. Becker had lost weight. Her green T-shirt hung loose on sharp shoulders, her arms looked bony and thin, her pale cheeks were hollowed, and she stared at Elly through faded blue eyes that now seemed too large for her thin face.

"Hi Mrs. Becker!" Elly did her best to sound chipper. "It's me, Elly Rose!"

Mrs. Becker stared at her with no sign of recognition.

"Elly Rose Frankel!" Elly said.

Mrs. Becker looked past Elly to her parents, then back at Elly.

"Why are you here?" she asked.

"I brought you this." Elly held out the plastic container. "It's cherry pie!"

Mrs. Becker took the plastic container and stared at it as if she had no idea what she was looking at. She shook her head and asked again, "Why are you here?"

"We brought *pie!*" Elly said, even though she knew that wasn't the answer Stuey's mom wanted.

Elly's dad forced a smile and said, "Anne, we just stopped by to see how you're doing. Elly wanted to bring you pie."

Mrs. Becker's eyes became small and glittery. She stabbed a forefinger toward Elly.

"Why is *she* still *here?*" Her voice rose and cracked on the word *here*.

Elly's mom grabbed Elly's shoulders and pulled her back. Her dad stepped in front her.

"Anne. I was thinking . . . I was wondering if I could give you a hand with your yard."

"My *yard?*" It came out like a snarl. "What's *wrong* with my *yard?*"

"Nothing, I just thought—"

"You bring me *pie?*"

"Anne—"

Mrs. Becker stepped forward and shouted, "*Bring me my son!*"

Elly's mom was pulling her back off the steps. Her dad held up his hands and said, "Anne, please . . ." There was a moment when Elly thought Mrs. Becker was going to jump on him, but the moment passed. Mrs. Becker froze, her face going hard and still.

"Get out," she said. "Leave. Me. Alone."

"Okay, okay, we're going." The three of them backed away, then turned and walked quickly back to the car. Mrs. Becker stood on the steps watching them until they were all in the car, then drew her arm back and threw the pie. The plastic container hit the windshield and burst open, covering the glass with gloopy, too-sweet cherry filling.

"Do you think we should call someone?" Elly's mom said as they drove home.

Her father was running the wipers, turning them on and off, spraying the windshield with wiper fluid. "I don't know . . . she isn't hurting anybody, and she wants to be left alone." He gave the windshield another spray. One cherry was stuck high on the glass where the wipers didn't reach. Elly couldn't take her eyes off it.

"Doesn't she have any relatives?" her mom said.

"I don't think so. Her parents are gone, and she had no siblings. Maybe she just needs time to work things out."

"It's been a year."

"I know."

The cherry was slowly sliding down the windshield. Finally it slid low enough for the wipers to get it, but her dad had turned them off.

"Maybe we should call her doctor. Or social services."

"Maybe. I just keep thinking it could be us. I mean, if it had been Elly, would you want a bunch of doctors and social workers banging on our door?"

Elly, watching the cherry slide down the glass, knew there was only one thing that could help Mrs. Becker. For Stuey to come back.

grimpus

The dragons and the elves were waging war beneath swirling gray skies. The dragons' distant bellows and roars swept up the forested hillside, shivering the leaves, mounting the stockade, and spilling into the garden where the Queen of the Wood sat on her royal divan, listening. The elvish warriors clattered and buzzed and trilled.

Grimpus sat on her lap, ears back, tail lashing. Grimpus was not fond of dragons. He hated everything and everyone except the queen herself.

The dragons fell silent. A moment later there came a splintering sound, and a dull crash. The dragons snarled in triumph.

"They're knocking down the trees, Grimpy," said the queen.

Grimpus did not reply. The queen lifted her chalice to her lips and sipped. The sweet nectar had turned bitter from sorrow. She scowled and set it aside.

"One day, Grimpy, I will escape these walls and reclaim my kingdom. I swear it on the lost soul of my knight-in-waiting."

The dragons started roaring again, followed by the thunder of more dragons calling from beyond the horizon. The queen tried to imagine the elvish armies doing battle. She put her hands over her ears and squeezed her eyes shut. It was hard. Too hard to picture them. The image was fuzzy and distant and not at all real.

The dragons were bulldozers. The elves were birds and cicadas and buzzing flies, her sweet nectar was apple juice, and Grimpus had no ears.

A drop of rain fell from the sky and struck the tip of her nose.

"Elly!" The strident voice cut through her hands and drilled into her ears. She did not respond. Another raindrop struck the corner of her eye and ran down her cheek.

"Come inside! It's raining!"

Grimpus fell from her lap to the stone patio and stared up at the gray sky through one yellow glass eye.

"Elly Rose! Now!"

Elly sighed and sat up on the chaise longue. Her mother was looking at her from the back door. Large raindrops spotted the patio tiles between them. Elly stood up wordlessly. She did not want to get wet, but she also didn't want to go inside just because her mom said so.

"They're wrecking the woods," she said.

"It's just a few trees," her mother said. "They're clearing them out for the new lake."

"I don't want a stupid boring lake."

Mrs. Frankel rolled her eyes.

"Don't leave your cat out there. He'll get wet."

Elly bent over and grabbed Grimpus by one floppy fabric leg.

"Don't you think you're getting a little too old for dolls?"

"He's not a doll. He's Grimpus."

"Why don't you let me run him through the wash for you?"

The rain was coming harder. Elly looked at the tattered gray cat hanging from her hand. His ears had been worn to nubs and his remaining eye hung by a thread. White fuzz spilled from the seam on his belly.

"Cats don't like baths," she said.

deluge

Weeks later, during the hottest part of August, Elly Rose stuffed Grimpus into her backpack and headed out into the woods. The air was utterly still. Clouds of gnats hovered over the path. She could hear the lazy buzzing of bees, occasionally interrupted by the rattle and hiss of cicadas, and a distant roar and rumble.

"Don't worry, Grimpy," she said. "It's not dragons. Just stupid men and their stupid machines."

Grimpus did not reply. Every day it got harder to pretend.

She reached the bottom of the wooded slope. Tomorrow, everything would be different. This would be the edge of a lake. But for now it was dry. Before her lay devastation, nothing but broken trunks and crushed undergrowth.

"It's okay, Grimpy," she said to reassure herself. "They won't open the dam until tomorrow."

There would be a ceremony. The mayor would be there, along with her parents and all the other members of the preservation society. This was her last chance to visit the Castle Rose—ever.

It took a long time to get there. She had to climb over or around the fallen trees. Her backpack kept getting caught on branches. When the Castle Rose finally came into view, she stopped and stared. The deadfall had collapsed.

What had once been a grand pyramidal shape now looked like a pile of logs with one long limb sticking up like a crooked flagpole. Elly approached cautiously and peered through the tangle of branches and tree trunks. She found an opening and wriggled inside. There wasn't enough room to stand, even bent over. One of the biggest trunks had crashed down on the stone slab. Elly recalled the last time she had been there, how the slab had tried to grab her. She felt a chill run through her. *Don't be silly,* she told herself. *It was a dream.*

She thought about Stuey. Maybe everything that had happened was a dream, a hallucination, a fairy tale she had invented. Because rocks don't really grow fingers of stone, and dragons are just bulldozers made of metal. People don't disappear into thin air. There are no such things as ghosts.

It was time to stop pretending. Time to grow up.

She pulled Grimpus from her backpack and set him on the stone. "Sorry, Grimpy."

Back outside, she took one last look at the fallen Castle Rose.

It's just a pile of dead trees, she told herself. *Tomorrow they will be gone forever.*

As soon as she turned her back on the deadfall, Elly felt two conflicting emotions: sadness and relief. It was the same way she'd felt three years ago when her real cat, Meowster, died after several weeks of piteous meowing. Meowster had been seventeen years old. Instead of a new cat, her mom had given her Grimpus. Now it was Grimpy's time, and the castle's time. It seemed only right that they should go together.

Walking slowly, she headed for home. As she neared the pond she noticed rivulets of water flowing across the path. She had never seen that before except when it was raining. She looked up at the cloudless sky. Where was the water coming from? The path became wetter. Puddles were forming, growing larger before her eyes. Soon she was sloshing through ankle-deep water.

Elly came to a tree that had been cut down. She

climbed onto the trunk and looked toward the highway. Even though it was more than a quarter mile away, she could see men moving around frantically by the dam, and the glint of the sun reflecting from water where there had been no water before. The creek had broken through the dam.

The water was returning to Westdale Wood.

Elly jumped off the trunk and landed with a splash. She started running. If she could reach the hill below her neighborhood, she'd be safe. It wasn't that far — normally she could get there in a few minutes — but she had all those fallen trees in the way, and the rising water was making it hard to run. She couldn't see what she was stepping on. She had only gone about fifty feet when she tripped on an underwater branch and fell face-first.

I'm going to drown, she thought, spitting out swampy-tasting water. She got up and kept going, her pulse drumming in her ears. The water got deeper with every step she took. It was up to her shins when she saw a groundhog claw its way out of the water onto a fallen tree. It crouched there, sodden and frightened, watching her as she splashed past.

By the time she reached the bottom of the hill she was wading through water up to her hips. She dragged herself, soaked and muddy, up onto the leaf-covered slope.

Behind her, the water continued to rise.

At dinner that night, Elly's dad was furious.

"What a mess." He stabbed a meatball with his fork and ate it in one bite.

He wasn't talking about Elly—she had made it home hours ago, cleaned herself up, and put on dry clothes. She didn't want her parents to know she'd almost drowned. They always got mad at her when she got hurt, or even almost hurt.

He was upset about the dam.

"A complete and utter catastrophe. The plan was to flood the lake slowly, and it wasn't supposed to happen until tomorrow. Some fool lost control of his earthmover and the dam collapsed. Now we have no way to control the water level."

"Will peoples' houses get flooded?" Elly asked.

"I doubt it. The lake will stabilize at its historic level, which is what we'd always planned. But a big storm could create problems—we need to rebuild the dam to keep the lake level steady. The preservation society will be blamed if anything happens."

"What about the animals?"

"What about them?"

"Do you think they drowned?"

"I'm sure they're okay, honey," said her mother.

"What about the baby groundhogs down in their holes?"

"I don't know," her father said. "That was one of the reasons we wanted to flood the lake in stages, to give the wildlife a chance to adapt. It was an accident."

"When I do something and say it was an accident I get punished!"

"This was not your father's fault, Elly," her mother said.

"When I say something's not my fault you—"

"Elly Rose!" her mother snapped.

Elly closed her mouth and looked down at her spaghetti and meatballs. She'd pushed the meatballs aside because she'd been thinking about the animals. Now she wasn't hungry at all.

"And Stuey," she muttered.

"What?" her mother asked.

"Stuey could be out there too."

Her parents looked at her, but they did not know what to say.

crushed

After school let out for the summer, Stuey convinced Deshan to come with him to the deadfall. Deshan hadn't been much interested until Stuey mentioned that it was the place where Elly Rose Frankel had disappeared. Deshan had never known Elly, but he'd heard about her and he'd seen her on the billboards so he thought maybe it would be cool.

Deshan did not like the woods. He had grown up in Minneapolis where the streets were a grid and there were stores on every corner.

"These trees must be a thousand years old," he said. "Like they're ready to keel over on us."

"Actually, most of them are only sixty or seventy years old," Stuey told him. "This used to be a golf course, and my family owned it. My great-grandfather built it. He was a bootlegger."

"Seriously? What's a bootlegger?"

"Like a smuggler."

"Like a gangster?"

"I guess so. He smuggled whiskey during Prohibition. But then he went straight and built the golf course." Stuey told him about how his great-grandfather and Robert Rosen had disappeared on the same night.

"They never found them?" Deshan asked.

"Not a trace. My grandpa used to say their ghosts are still out here."

Deshan gave him a doubtful look. "Yeah, right."

"I'm not saying I believed him."

They followed the trail through a patch of nettles, holding up their arms so they wouldn't get stung. Stuey hadn't been in the woods for weeks, and the path was getting overgrown.

"This is crazy," Deshan said. "Are there snakes?"

"No, but Elly said there were bears and alligators out here."

"Vampires too, I bet." Deshan slapped a mosquito. "Bloodsuckers. It's like a jungle. You ever get lost? Maybe that girl is still trying to find her way out of here."

"It's not that big," Stuey said.

"I hope they build that mall soon."

"Wait till you see the deadfall," Stuey said. "It's really cool."

"Whatever," Deshan said.

When they got there a few minutes later, Deshan was not impressed.

"It's a pile of dead trees," he said. "So what?"

Stuey had to admit, the deadfall didn't look as impressive as it used to. It seemed to have sagged a bit. He pointed at the opening. "We can go inside."

"It looks like it's about to fall down."

"Don't be a wuss. Come on." Stuey ducked inside.

A few seconds later, Deshan poked his head in.

"I don't want to get crushed."

"You won't get crushed."

Deshan entered.

"This is it?" he said doubtfully.

"Elly Frankel called it the Castle Rose."

"You made up a name for it? That's lame."

"I was sitting right here when she disappeared."

He had told Deshan about it before. Deshan hadn't believed him then, and he didn't believe him now.

"Yeah, right. Like she got caught in a transporter beam? Give me a break." He looked around. "Kind of creepy though."

"I used to think it was magic."

Deshan laughed. "You believe in the Easter Bunny too?"

"I mean, I thought it was magic when I was a little kid."

"Yeah, right." Deshan smirked.

"Mostly it was Elly who thought it was magic," Stuey said, then felt bad for blaming it on her.

Deshan kicked at the floor. "It's really dirty in here. Like grimy beach sand."

"I think it's an old sand trap from when it was a golf course."

"What's with the rock? How'd that get here?"

"I don't know."

Deshan shook his head. "Creepy. Creepy and dirty. Let's get out of here."

Stuey went by himself after that, but less often. He still heard the voices and heard the music, but it was very faint. The deadfall felt different now. Maybe Deshan was right. Magic was for little kids.

He was thinking about that as he trudged through the woods alone on the anniversary of Elly's disappearance. He hadn't been to the deadfall in two weeks. He felt guilty for not going, and he was angry about feeling guilty. Why should he feel bad? He'd been there dozens of times over the summer, and every time he felt stupid. Like Deshan was looking over his shoulder laughing at him. So he got mad at Deshan. And he was mad at Elly Rose for never being there. And at the people who were going to build the mall. And at himself. Why did he bother? He didn't even like being there anymore.

Deshan was right. It was creepy. Creepy and dirty, and darker than he remembered.

Stuey sat on the slab. Before, being there had relaxed him, but now he was all jagged inside. He stood up and hit his head on a branch. Either the deadfall was settling or he was getting taller. He grabbed the branch and tried to snap it off. It wouldn't budge. He took out his Swiss Army knife and used the tiny saw blade to cut halfway through, then grasped it with both hands and threw his weight against it. The branch snapped and he fell, his head bouncing off the slab.

He jumped up, suddenly furious, and yanked at the branches above him. The limb he was pulling on gave way; he fell back. Creaking and groaning, the deadfall collapsed. One of the cottonwood trunks hammered down, pinning him to the slab. Stuey gasped as the trunk compressed his chest. He felt as if his ribs were about to crack. He had no air and he could not scream.

plus fours

It felt like an eternity. The massive trunk squeezed him against the slab. He could breathe, but only in tiny gasps—enough to stay alive, but not enough to shout for help. Not that anyone would hear him.

I'm going to die, he thought.

The Castle Rose was killing him. He closed his eyes and concentrated on breathing, each sip of air a small fraction of a breath. He counted each one; they sounded like hiccups. Then he heard a voice.

"Hang in there, son."

His grandfather's voice—but that was impossible.

"Help is coming."

It *was* Gramps!

"Gramps?" he squeaked. There was no reply.

Stuey kept breathing. It took all his strength, and with every scanty, meager breath the trunk pressed down harder.

"Somebody in there?" A man's voice, not his grandfather.

Stuey tried to yell. All that came out was a wheezy rasp. It was enough.

"Are you stuck?" He heard branches breaking. A moment later he saw a face peering in at him. He knew that face.

"Can you breathe?" the man asked.

Stuey shook his head. More breaking branches.

"I'm gonna get a lever under here, son. Don't think I can raise that trunk up much, but maybe just enough. You feel the pressure ease up, you slide on out. You think you can do that?"

Stuey nodded. The man had a branch about four inches thick. He wedged it under the trunk.

"You ready?"

Stuey nodded. The man heaved up on the branch. Veins stood out on his neck. The trunk shifted slightly, but not enough. The man stopped lifting and the trunk settled even lower, forcing the last bit of air from Stuey's lungs.

Black bubbles crowded the edges of his vision. He heard the man say, "Hang on, let me try down here."

The trunk shifted again, but this time the pressure eased. Stuey gasped and air flooded his lungs.

"Now, son! Slide on out!"

Stuey kicked and twisted. The trunk scraped against his chest. He pushed against it with his hands and wriggled out from beneath it. He was free. The man let go of the branch and the trunk crashed down onto the slab. He grabbed Stuey and pulled him out of the deadfall. When the man let go, Stuey fell to his knees and sucked in great ragged lungfuls of air, heedless of the sharp pains from his ribs.

"You okay?" the man asked.

"I think so." It hurt to talk.

The man was dressed all in camouflage. On the ground next to him was a wicker basket full of yellow mushrooms.

"You're the Mushroom Man," Stuey said.

The man laughed. "I prefer Greg," he said.

"I thought you moved away."

"I did, but I came back just this once. Next year this place will be all concrete and steel. I figure this is my last chance to pick chanterelles here." He pointed at the yellow mushrooms in his basket. "They're delicious."

"Oh."

"You're very lucky," the man said. "I'm lucky too. If you'd died in there, they might never have found you and they'd try to blame me again." He narrowed his eyes. "You're the kid who took my picture, aren't you?"

Stuey nodded.

"That girl . . . she was your friend?"

"Elly Rose," Stuey said.

"You know I had nothing to do with her disappearing, right?"

"I never said you did."

They both looked at the pile of dead trees.

"How did you know to find me?" Stuey asked.

"It was rather odd." The man shrugged nervously. "I was picking mushrooms and all of a sudden there's this guy standing in front of me. Some old dude in a ratty sweater, smoking a pipe. I don't know where he came from. He told me there was a boy trapped in the deadfall."

Gramps. Stuey's heart was racing, each beat causing a twinge in his ribs.

"Where is he?" he managed to ask.

"I don't know. I looked where he was pointing and when I turned back he was gone. Like he'd evaporated. Kind of spooky, if you ask me. These woods . . . I don't know. I never feel all that comfortable out here."

"Do you ever hear the music?" Stuey asked.

The man looked startled. "You hear that too?"

"And the voices?"

The man licked his lips and looked behind him nervously. "Sometimes."

"Do you ever see Elly Rose?"

"No! But I've seen . . . well, one time I thought I saw a man in a suit talking to a guy wearing plus fours. Nobody's worn plus fours since before I was born."

"Plus what?"

"Plus fours. Old-fashioned golf pants. Like baggy knickers. I just saw the two men for a second, and I blinked and they were gone." He spat out a nervous laugh. "I don't believe in ghosts, but if I did, this is the place for them. Maybe turning it into a mall isn't such a bad idea."

bruised

Stuey's mom saw them coming across the orchard. She must have seen that Stuey was walking funny. She ran across the yard and grabbed him by the shoulders.

"Are you all right?"

"I think so."

"He had a little mishap." The Mushroom Man held out his hand. "Greg Eagen."

She shook his hand. "Aren't you . . ."

"Yeah, that's me. I was hunting mushrooms. Your son got himself stuck under a log. I helped him out."

"I was in the deadfall," Stuey said.

"Oh, Stuey!" His mom hugged him, then let go when Stuey yelped.

"You might want to have a doctor take a look at those ribs." The Mushroom Man picked up his basket. "I'll be going now. Just wanted to make sure the boy got home okay."

"Thank you," she said. Stuey could tell she wasn't too sure about him.

"Yeah, thanks," Stuey said.

The man touched the brim of his camouflage hat and walked back through the orchard and into the woods.

On the way to the urgent care clinic, Stuey told his mom a version of what had happened. He tried to make it sound like no big deal, but of course she said, "You could have been killed!"

"I probably could have got out myself," he said, even though he knew it wasn't true.

"No more going in that woods alone," she said.

Stuey didn't argue. It hurt his chest to talk, and at the moment he didn't want to go in the woods ever again.

The doctor was the same one who'd seen him a year ago when he got the concussion.

"Another Tarzan mishap?" the doctor asked.

Stuey told him what had happened. The doctor examined him. They took some X-rays. It turned out his ribs weren't broken.

"Just some nasty bruising," the doctor said. "You'll be sore for a few days."

"It doesn't hurt that bad," Stuey said, even though it did.

The doctor laughed. "I'm sure you'll be back to performing hazardous stunts in no time."

That night his mom was getting ready to go to another preservation society meeting. They had succeeded in getting the construction delayed until next year—something about an environmental impact study—but the mall seemed to be inevitable. The meeting was to discuss future options. Nobody thought it would do much good.

"If I wasn't the president of the society I probably wouldn't go," Stuey's mom said with a sigh. "But I guess I have to go through the motions. Daddy would want me to. The truth is, I joined mostly because I thought it was what he'd want."

"Do you think Gramps knows?"

"Do you mean is he watching from heaven?"

"Or someplace."

She laughed. "I wouldn't put it past him. If anything still connects him to this life it's those woods. All the time I was growing up he talked about buying it back, but we never had the money."

"Do you think Grandpa Zach is a ghost?"

"I think he lives on in our memories, and in the things he left behind."

"You mean like his pipes?"

"All of his things—the trees he planted, the clothes still hanging in his closet, that book he was working on . . ."

Stuey had all but forgotten about Grandpa Zach's book—the hundreds of yellow pages they had gathered up after the storm that had killed him.

"His *Book of Secrets*," Stuey said. "Can I read it?"

She put down her fork and looked him right in the eyes. "Stuey, those pages were in pretty bad shape. I don't even know why we tried to save them. Sometimes secrets are secrets for a reason—best to let them lie." She looked at the clock. "I'd better get going. Are you going to be okay here for a couple of hours?"

"I'll just watch TV." Since he turned ten, his mom had been letting him stay home alone sometimes.

As soon as she left he went upstairs to his grandfather's room and opened the door.

secrets

Grandpa Zach's room had been untouched since Stuey and his mom had stored his papers there two years ago. Enough dust had sifted in through the cracks to leave a fine, whitish layer upon every horizontal surface. The spiders had been at work too — delicate, chaotic strands of webbing filled the corners and crannies, giving everything a soft, gauzy look.

Stuey stood in the doorway for almost a minute wondering if he really wanted to do this. It felt as if he was about to step inside the skeleton of his grandfather's life.

He took a breath and went in. The cobwebs near him shivered. He saw no spiders — they had died off, or given up and left for lack of insects to eat. The silence pressed on his eardrums; the dryness of the air pinched his nose.

The Moroccan sword still hung on the wall above the bed. Black-and-white dead people stared out from the framed photos. On the bed, the cardboard box where they had put Gramps's pages was covered with a fine layer of dust. Thin strands of frosted cobweb drooped from the edge of the box to the bedposts. Stuey brushed away the webbing. The brittle tape holding the box shut came loose with a dry crackle. He opened the flaps.

Inside, the top page was covered with black, powdery mildew. He picked it up and shook it. The resulting cloud of spores made him sneeze. He looked at the page. He could make out the ghost of Grandpa Zach's uneven scrawl, but it was too damaged to read.

The next page was better, but he could only read a few lines. Something about planting apple trees. He leafed through the top several pages. Water damage, mold, and mildew had rendered them unreadable. He lifted the pile of papers out of the box and slowly went through them. Every so often he would find a page that was partially legible.

. . . *that summer Mother met with the lawyers every day, or so it seemed. We'd let the grounds crew go, so it was just me and Chico trying to keep the course in shape. We closed the back nine that July. Membership*

was down to eighty-four. Mom said we needed twice
that many members to stay in business. I suggested
selling off all but nine holes and the clubhouse, but
Mother was still convinced that Pop would show up
someday and fix everything. Some nights I heard her
in her bedroom talking. I think she was talking to Pop,
asking him what we should do. If so, he didn't tell her
anything very useful, because by September of that
year we had to close the course for good.

No secrets there. He found a page covered with
numbers that didn't make any sense at first. A secret
code? After a few minutes he figured out it was just a list
of dates and golf scores. No secrets there either.

A third page contained a legible fragment that made
the back of his neck all prickly.

. . . believe that every possible future exists and we
all exist within a great tangled and frayed tapestry
of potentiality. There are many worlds — as many
worlds as there are thoughts. My father is playing golf
in his world while in my world he is dead and gone.
The question is, once one world becomes two, can
the two worlds ever be brought back together? Is that
what happens when I see you, Pop? Are you really
there, or are you a figment of my imagination?

The rest of the page was too water damaged to read. Stuey went through the rest of the box. Only a dozen or so pages were legible, and most of those were about ordinary things: how many apple trees he had planted, part of a story about his dog getting sprayed by a skunk, and an account of his daughter Annie's thirteenth birthday party. He had given her a Walkman, whatever that was, and a gift certificate to Dayton's, a store Stuey had never heard of.

He found one more fragment of interest.

. . . is the truth more powerful than hatred and lies? If so, then shared truth must be more powerful still. Can the truth bring together that which is broken? Can it mend a shattered reality? I am too much the coward to ever know. I dared to record my secrets only because I knew they would not be read until I died, and perhaps not even . . .

Stuey sighed and piled the pages back in the box. If there had ever been secrets in there, they would stay secret.

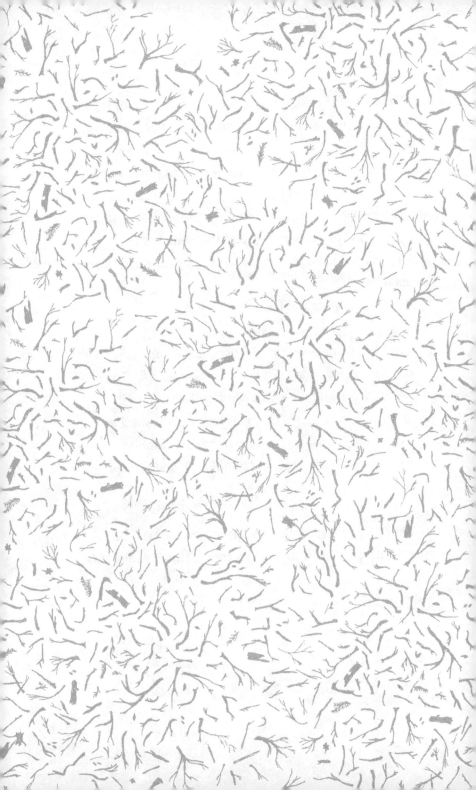

the notebook

good-bye

On the morning of his eleventh birthday, Stuey was awakened by a series of loud, rhythmic bangs. He opened his window and stuck his head outside. The banging was coming from over by the highway, where a crane was driving steel pilings into the marshy earth. Much closer, from just the other side of the poplar grove, came the whining buzz of chain saws and the growling of bulldozers. Stuey dressed and went downstairs.

On the kitchen table was a frosted bran muffin with two candles stuck in it, and a card from his mom. The card had a drawing of a bright-red cardinal. A word balloon coming from the bird's beak read:

Wake Up, Sleepyhead! It's Your Birthday!

Below that was a note telling him that she'd run to the store and would be back in an hour. He sat at the table and ate the muffin and thought about the deadfall. It had been almost a year since he'd been there—the time he'd almost died. Since then he had hardly been in the woods at all. It was too depressing knowing that soon it would all be gone and he would never see Elly again.

Ever.

He was eleven now, far too old to believe in such things as fairies and ghosts and people who disappear. For most of the past year he had tried not to think about her, and when he did, it was like remembering a distant dream. Most days he thought he'd made the whole thing up. That was what his mom thought. It was what everybody thought.

Westdale was forgetting about Elly Rose too. Elly's dad had stopped paying for the billboards. Elly's picture was replaced by car ads. The Frankels put their house up for sale. They were moving to Atlanta. All anybody talked about was Westdale Mall, set to open next year.

Stuey finished the muffin, licked the frosting off the candles, and put the plate in the sink.

Most of the woods was gone already. The higher areas were being leveled and the low areas filled. Two weeks ago the bulldozers and earthmovers had arrived, eating away at the edges of the woods like ants attacking a cookie, moving in toward the center, toward the Castle Rose.

The main reason Stuey hadn't been there was because he didn't want to remember. Elly had left a hole in his gut, an emptiness that he could not bear to look at. He had new friends now—Deshan and Heck and Alison Quist and a few others . . . but it wasn't the same. Not even close.

The first time he met Elly, she had told him he was shy. It was true. With Alison he always found himself looking off to the side, avoiding her eyes. And with Deshan and Heck he was always faking it, pretending to be more grown up than he felt. Elly had been different. He could look straight into her eyes and say whatever he wanted.

He didn't want to think about Elly. Usually he could push her to the back of his mind, wall her off, build a hard shell around her. But not today. Today was her birthday too.

He went upstairs to his room and opened the desk drawer and found the compass Elly had given him. He hadn't looked at it since last summer. He put his head through the shoelace and tucked the compass under his shirt, close to his heart.

Today, he would have to say good-bye.

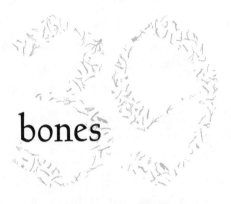

bones

The oak knoll had been sliced in half, right on the property line. Beyond, what had once been a rolling landscape crowded with trees was a flattened wasteland. Broken trees were piled along the far side, waiting to be trucked away. The only thing left was the deadfall, right at the center of the expanse.

An excavator with a claw bucket approached the deadfall. Its steel claw bit into one of the cottonwood trunks, shook it, and ripped it free. Stuey imagined the sucking sound of bone being pulled from flesh, like a vulture tearing at roadkill.

The deadfall sagged. The excavator swung the trunk onto the waiting flatbed truck.

Stuey raised his eyes to the fringe of trees on the far side of the devastation.

He could see a faint crease in the denuded hillside, all that remained of the ravine where he'd hit his head. He put his hand to his chest and felt the compass beneath his shirt.

It only took a few minutes for the excavator to load the last trunk onto the truck.

The guy on the excavator climbed off and walked over to where the deadfall had been. The truck driver joined him.

They were looking at the slab, Stuey realized. He wanted to yell at them to leave it alone, but they were too far away. He leaned forward and almost fell off the edge of the cut. Don't be stupid, he told himself, backing away. If he ran out there and told them to leave the rock alone they'd think he was crazy. Maybe he *was* crazy.

It's just a rock, he told himself.

The Castle Rose was gone.

Elly Rose was gone.

There was nothing he could do.

The two men stood over the slab talking. After a minute, one of them climbed back on the excavator. The other man stood back.

The excavator eased forward. The claw bucket bit into the earth, wedged under the edge of the slab, and slowly raised it up. Stuey stopped breathing. The slab tipped up, slid off the bucket, and cracked in two.

The operator climbed off his machine. Both men ran over to look at what they had uncovered.

Stuey skidded down the dirt embankment and ran headlong across the field of dirt and mud and wood chips, leaping over shredded stumps and water-filled tractor tracks. He wasn't thinking, he had no idea what he would do when he got there, no sense of why he was running. He only knew he couldn't stand and watch anymore.

The men saw him coming and waved their arms, signaling him to go back. Stuey ignored them. Moments later he came to a stop at the edge of the rectangular depression where the stone slab had been. One of the men was yelling at him to back away. Stuey ignored him and tried to climb down into the depression. The man grabbed his arm and pulled him back, but not before Stuey saw what had been hidden beneath the slab — a layer of dirty white sand with black mud oozing up through it, and something else. He shook off the man's grip and fell to his knees, his head spinning.

The truck driver said, "Are you all right, kid?"

Stuey shook his head and crawled toward the hole. The man grabbed him again.

"Son, you can't go in there. The police won't want you messing things up."

"I have to see," Stuey said.

"It's just some old animal bones is all."

But he had seen clearly, among the naked, yellowing bones, a crushed rib cage—and a human skull.

all wet

The truck driver was on his phone, talking excitedly. Stuey and the other man stood a few yards back from the hole. He couldn't see inside, but he knew what he'd seen.

"Didn't some kid go missing a few years back?" the excavator operator asked.

Stuey nodded.

The truck driver pocketed his phone and said, "Summer before last. I was out here searching for her along with half the town." He shook his head. "Poor kid."

"Wonder if that's her," the excavator operator said.

"Who knows?"

Stuey edged back toward the hole. The men didn't try to stop him. He looked down at the rib cage and the broken skull. A shadow passed over the bones. He looked up.

Elly Rose was floating five feet above the hole, her legs out in front of her, as if she was sitting on an invisible magic carpet. She was wearing a puffy life jacket and holding a two-bladed paddle.

"Elly," Stuey said. He started toward her, but it was hard to move. The air abruptly turned to water, neck deep, and he saw that Elly was in a small boat—a kayak. He pushed forward, splashing with his arms. The bottom dropped from beneath him and he went under. He clawed his way to the surface, coughing and spitting. Elly's face was only a few feet away, looking at him wide-eyed. He reached out for her, but something grabbed his other wrist. He was being pulled back, then up, and suddenly he was on dry ground.

"What the heck, kid, are you crazy?"

He was standing next to the hole, dripping wet. The truck driver was gripping his wrist. The water was gone. Elly was gone.

"Look, kid, something bad happened here, and the cops aren't going to want your footprints all over. What's the matter with you?"

"What happened?" Stuey asked.

"You jumped in that hole, son." The truck driver let go of his arm.

Stuey could see his footprints in the dirt—with the bones.

"He's soaking wet, Bob," the truck driver said.

"No kidding. How'd you get so wet, kid?"

Stuey looked around. Everything else was dry—including the two men—but he was completely drenched. His shoes were covered with sticky black mud.

"I have no idea," he said.

The men stared at him, at the water running off him, puddling at his feet.

"Weird," said the truck driver.

kayak

That morning Elly had awakened to a familiar feeling. Her father was standing at the foot of her bed wiggling her toes. She groaned, pulled her feet back under the covers, and wrapped her pillow over her head.

"Up and at 'em, sleepyhead. Mom and I want to give you your present before I leave for work."

"Present?" Elly peeked out at him.

"It's your birthday, silly!"

Elly sat up. Her birthday! She hopped out of bed and dressed quickly. What had they gotten her? A new computer, maybe? Clothes? She hoped it wasn't clothes—her mom always wanted her to dress like a little girl. Maybe they'd gotten her a kitten. A real one.

Her mom was in the kitchen making waffles. Elly loved waffles.

"Happy birthday, sweetie!"

Elly looked around for her present.

"Out on the patio," her mom said.

Elly slid open the patio door. Her dad was standing beside a bright-red, eight-foot-long kayak with a giant pink bow around it.

"Happy birthday, sweetie," her dad said.

"You got me a boat," Elly said.

"A kayak!" her dad said.

Elly didn't trust herself to say anything. She forced herself to smile.

"It's great! You'll love it!" He held up a two-bladed paddle and an orange life jacket. "For the new lake!"

"Oh." Elly had been determined to hate the new lake and everything about it. "Um . . . thank you?"

"You're welcome! I'll help you lug it down after breakfast."

"I thought you had to go to work."

"Don't worry, we have plenty of time."

At first she stayed close to shore. Her dad stood at the edge of the lake and watched as she struggled to get the hang of the paddle.

"You got it," he yelled.

She paddled backward on one side to turn the kayak. It was easier than she thought. The tiny boat was a little tippy, but she wasn't worried about capsizing because she had the life jacket. She pointed the front of the kayak away from shore.

"Don't go out too far!" her dad yelled.

Elly aimed the prow at a dark tree limb sticking out of the water in the middle of the lake.

"Elly!"

She ignored him and paddled toward the lone deadhead. The kayak skimmed across the lake. She soon reached the deadhead. She stopped, waited for the ripples to settle down, and peered down through the water at the dark trunks and branches that had once been the Castle Rose.

"Grimpy? Are you still there?" She imagined him tangled in the branches. "I'm sorry I drowned you." She blinked back tears, then laughed at herself. Grimpy was an old ragged stuffed doll, a child's toy. She dipped one end of the paddle into the water to turn the kayak around, then hesitated and looked back down at the submerged deadfall.

Something was moving, rising toward her. An instant later it exploded up out of the water—a boy, gasping and flailing with his arms.

Stuey! They locked eyes, but before either of them could say anything he sank.

Elly leaned over the edge of the kayak, trying to see through the rippled surface. Had she really seen him? The widening ripples from his splashing faded. Stuey was gone. Was he down there someplace? She leaned out farther, then jerked back as the kayak threatened to capsize.

She had seen him. He had seen her too—she was sure of it.

She waited.

"Come back," she said. The lake absorbed her small voice.

Her dad was yelling at her from across the lake. She waved to let him know she was okay, then continued looking down into the water.

All she could see were the submerged remains of Castle Rose, sodden and dark.

there is more

Stuey hung around until the police came and shooed him off. He walked home slowly, thoughts whirling through his head. Had those bones been Elly's? If they were, then had he seen her ghost? Had he imagined it? But if it had been all in his head, then how had he gotten soaked? He hadn't imagined *that*. His shoes were still squelching and his jeans were wet.

If it *had* been real, what was Elly doing in a kayak? And she had looked different—her hair was longer and she looked older. Did ghosts age?

Nothing made sense. He had thought he would be saying good-bye to Elly Rose, but it was more like they had said hello all over again. He pulled out his compass and looked at it. It was full of water. Probably ruined.

As he crossed the orchard he picked a green apple. He bit into the bitter flesh, spat it out, and threw it away.

The worst thing was that he couldn't talk to anybody about it. His mom might send him back to Dr. Missou. Deshan and Heck would laugh at him. Alison would tell him he was being stupid.

He wished Grandpa Zach was still around. Gramps would listen. He might even believe him, or at least pretend to.

Stuey stopped at Gramps's grave. It had been three years since they buried him. Green moss was creeping up the shaded side of the granite tombstone.

"I'm sorry we lost your woods," he said. "Mom tried really hard."

No reply — not that he expected one.

"They found a skeleton. Under a rock." He stared hard at the gravestone. "I guess you're under a rock too."

Gramps would have laughed.

"I tried to read your book. It was kind of messed up from the storm. I didn't find any secrets."

Things nobody knows, Grandpa Zach had once told him.

"Mom says secrets are secrets for a reason."

Things nobody would believe. He could almost hear his

grandfather's voice. He sniffed. Something was burning. It smelled like pipe tobacco. The back of his neck prickled.

"Look harder," Grandpa Zach said.

Stuey froze and his heart thumped. He couldn't move — it was as if the air around him had solidified and was holding him. It sounded like Gramps was standing right behind him.

"Gramps?" His voice came out a squeak.

"Read my book."

"Your book got wrecked in the storm." A curl of aromatic smoke drifted past Stuey's cheek. Gramps was close.

"There is more," Gramps said, right in his ear. Stuey closed his eyes tight. His breaths were coming fast and shallow; the smell of pipe tobacco was overwhelming; he could feel his heartbeat in his throat.

"My *Book of Secrets*." Gramps's voice now sounded farther away. "Look harder."

"Where?"

He heard his grandfather's laugh, then his cough. It seemed to be coming from deep in the orchard.

"Grandpa? Gramps?"

He could barely hear the reply: "Let me go, Stuey."

Suddenly he could move. He whirled around, looking

in every direction. He backed away from the grave and hugged himself, heart racing, goose bumps standing out on his arms.

It wasn't real, he told himself — but he could feel the impression of his grandfather's voice in his ears.

He could still smell the smoke.

book of secrets

The discovery of the bones was the first thing on the news that night.

"Construction workers made a grisly discovery at the site of the new mall in Westdale this morning. Reporting from the scene is Andrea Stevens."

The report cut to Westdale Wood, to a blond woman standing in front of a strip of yellow police tape. Behind her several policemen were milling around the broken slab and the shallow hole.

"Thank you, Cal. Police have yet to identify the human remains discovered here, but some are speculating that it could be Elly Rose Frankel, who was last seen at this exact spot two years ago this summer."

A picture of Elly flashed on the screen.

Stuey's mom clicked off the TV.

"You don't need to be watching this." She got up from the sofa. "I'll be in my studio."

Stuey's mom had been spending nearly all her time in her studio. She said it was therapeutic, whatever that meant. The Westdale Preservation Society had failed to save the woods, so she threw herself into her work. She was painting what she called her "death cards"—a collection of depressing greeting cards depicting American birds that had gone extinct in the last two hundred years—the ivory-billed woodpecker, the passenger pigeon, the great auk, the Carolina parakeet— she had a list.

Stuey sat on the sofa thinking. His mom was right. They would know soon enough. The police would figure it out. But he kept thinking about what he'd heard—or imagined he'd heard—in the orchard.

Look harder, Gramps had said.

Look for what? Where?

Stuey went up to Grandpa Zach's room. Nothing had changed. The box of unreadable secrets was where he'd left it. He opened the box and flipped through a few of the pages. Still unreadable. If there was more, where would it be?

He started with the closet. It was full of Gramps's

clothes, mostly Pendleton shirts and khaki pants. There were several boxes in the back of the closet. Stuey opened each of them; they were all stuffed with old clothes, including a pair of white golf shoes with dried mud still stuck to the metal spikes.

He backed out of the closet, closed the door, and turned to the bookcase. He ran his fingers across the spines and pulled one out at random: *Quantum Mechanics and the Many Worlds Theory*. It was full of big words and charts and diagrams that looked like gobbledygook. He wondered if Gramps had understood any of it.

The dresser held nothing but socks, underwear, sweaters, and some old watches. Gramps's smoking sweater—the one he had been wearing the day he died—was neatly folded in the bottom drawer. He looked under the bed and found a long canvas bag. Inside the bag was a fishing rod. He zipped the bag shut and sat on the bed, feeling a bit foolish. He wasn't even sure that what had happened in the orchard really happened.

His eyes landed on the old leather golf bag, the one that had belonged to his great-grandfather.

The clubs were ancient, with wooden shafts and leather-wrapped grips worn smooth. Stuey peered down into the bag. More spiderwebs. He unzipped the large pocket on the side. Inside was a clothbound note-book. On the cover was a label. BOOK OF SECRETS was

written on the label, then crossed out and replaced with
THE TREE FELL.

Stuey opened the notebook. Yellow, lined pages covered with Gramps's handwriting. The script was not spidery and cramped like Gramps's later writing; it was strong and clear. Gramps must have written it when he was younger.

Stuey sat on the bed and began to read.

it's a boy

June 30, 2006

    I was in the orchard this morning trimming dead branches off the Prairie Spy tree. Lois says there's no better apple for pie. I was up on a ladder sawing away when I felt a chill, like the cold breath from an open refrigerator on a hot day. I stopped what I was doing and climbed down to the ground. A man was standing a few feet away with his back to me, looking at the house.

    I couldn't see his face, but I knew it was Pop. He always wore those old-fashioned plus fours when he golfed. He had his golf cap on too, a white linen porkpie as outdated as his pants. The same clothes he'd been wearing the last time I saw him alive.

Pop's ghost never looks at me. I'm not sure he knows
I'm there.

"What are you looking at?" I asked him.

He didn't answer. He never does. I looked at the
house to see what he was staring at so intently, but saw
nothing unusual. When I looked back he was gone.

Moments later I heard Lois calling my name. She was
running toward me from the house, waving her arms.

"Annie just had her baby!" she shouted. "It's a boy!"

Stuey felt the hairs stand up on the back of his neck.
His mom's name was Annie. This page, these words, had
been written on the day he was born!

The next page was dated a few days later.

July 5, 2006

I have carried these secrets far too long.

My father began his life of crime during Prohibition.
Pop was a teenager when he stole a jug of white lightning
from the back of a moonshiner's Model A pickup truck.
He sold it for twenty-five cents. Soon he was bringing
trucks full of whiskey across the border from Canada
and had become one of the biggest bootleggers in the
Upper Midwest. His buddies in those days were mostly
gangsters, guys like Leon Gleckman, Kid Cann, and
Alvin Karpis.

By the time Prohibition was repealed in 1933, Pop had
become the subject of an intensive criminal investigation
run by a young district attorney named Robert Rosen.
Pop saw the writing on the wall and closed down his boot-
legging operation. Mother was pregnant with me by that
time, and Pop made the decision to become a legitimate
businessman . . .

Stuey was several pages into the notebook when he
heard the *clunk-ka-clunk* of his mom coming up the stairs.
He shoved the notebook back in the bag, ran out into the
hallway, and closed the door.

"Hey," his mom said as she reached the top of the
stairs. "What are you up to, besides standing there looking guilty?"

"Nothing," Stuey said.

She raised her eyebrows. "It's been awfully quiet up
here."

"I was reading."

"I see." Still with the suspicious look.

"I was just going downstairs." He walked past her and
ran down the stairs. A moment later he heard her clogs
clunking toward her bedroom at the end of the hall.

the bunker

Stuey wasn't able to get back to the notebook until that night while his mom was binge-watching some British TV show where all they do is talk. He took the notebook to his room and curled up in bed.

I started working at the golf course when I was ten, picking up balls on the driving range. Pop paid me five cents a bucket, which was good money in those days. Eventually I went to work with the groundskeepers. By the time I was fifteen they were letting me drive the tractor.

Some of those groundskeepers were kind of sketchy. Pop had hired a bunch of his old cronies from his bootlegging days. One of the sketchier guys, Stan, chewed tobacco and had the brownest teeth I'd ever seen, but he told me a lot of good stories from the old days.

"Always carried Gertie back in the day," he said, pulling an old revolver from his pocket, a short-barreled .38 with wooden grips worn shiny. "Still do. Keep her for varmints. Them groundhogs can mess up a fairway in no time."

I don't know if Stan ever shot any groundhogs, but he did shoot up a bar one night. Fortunately, nobody got hurt. The cops confiscated his pistol and threw him in jail. When he got out a couple months later, Pop gave him his job back.

"But no more guns, Stan."

"No problem there," Stan said. "That district attorney, he won't give Gertie back to me anyways. I bet he kept it for himself."

I still wonder if this whole terrible thing started with Stan's gun.

When Pop opened the country club he invited all the local bigwigs to join. The mayor of Westdale was given a free lifetime membership, as were several other politicians.

Robert Rosen, the district attorney, did not receive an invitation. Rosen and Pop had a lot of unpleasant history from back in Pop's bootlegging days, and I don't think Pop would have let him join the club even if Rosen hadn't been Jewish.

I must have been about ten the first time I saw Robert Rosen in person. He showed up at our house one day with several policemen and a search warrant. A tall, thin man with a slightly stooped posture, he made me think of a crane or some other long-legged bird. He wore horn-rimmed glasses, a dark suit, and a frown. Rosen and the police spent hours going through Pop's papers, turning his office upside down. Pop was livid, but there was nothing he could do. I don't know what they were looking for, but whatever it was they didn't find it, or so Pop said. I didn't know anything of Pop's past back then.

As I later learned, Robert Rosen was looking to make a name for himself. During Prohibition he had prosecuted hundreds of bootleggers, smugglers, and speakeasy operators. He was never able to catch Pop. Even after Prohibition came to an end, Rosen kept trying to bring charges against him, but nothing stuck. Pop had too many friends in high places.

For most of my childhood Pop split his time between running the golf course and defending himself in court. He didn't have a lot of time for Mother and me, or even for golf, a game he loved. About the only time he could get out on the course was in the evening, all by himself.

The last time I saw him was the summer before my senior year of high school. Mother had made chicken à la king casserole, one of Pop's favorites. Pop called to say he was going to play a few holes before dinner, so Mother put the casserole in the oven and we waited. Around eight o'clock or so she got tired of waiting and sent me out to fetch him.

By the time I found him the sun was almost gone. The air was heavy and still. Tree shadows striped the fairway from one side to the other. He was on the seventh hole, and he was not alone.

I saw him from the far end of the fairway. He was standing in the white-sand bunker in front of the green, talking to another man.

They were arguing—Pop had a golf club in one hand and was pounding its head in the sand. The other man was stabbing his finger at Pop's chest. Even from two hundred yards away I recognized Robert Rosen by his height and his stooped posture.

I had a bad feeling.

I started running toward them, but I was too late. Rosen took something out of his pocket and waved it in Pop's face. Pop lifted his club in both hands and brought it slashing down on Rosen's head. At the same moment, I heard a sharp bang, like a firecracker.

Rosen collapsed. I stopped running, shocked by what I had seen. Pop dropped the club and stood very still, then sank to his knees.

I stood there undecided for a few seconds. I knew Pop

wouldn't want me to see what he had done. What would I—or could I—say to him?

He was kneeling over Rosen, almost as if he was praying for him. I started toward them. It felt like the air was fighting me. Every step was an effort. By the time I reached the bunker Pop had slumped to his side, clutching his belly.

I called out. He turned his face toward me and lifted a hand—I couldn't tell if he was greeting me or waving me away—then his hand dropped and he became very still.

My pulse hammered at me, a dull, subsonic throbbing. Pop's shirt was dark with blood. I saw a gun in the sand near Rosen's hand. I forced myself to breathe. The air was like bitter honey and the sun squatted on the horizon and darkness crowded the edges of my vision.

I knew they were both dead. I don't know how I knew. Perhaps I sensed their souls abandoning their bodies. Or maybe it was the amount of blood seeping into the sand. Or their lack of movement, an utter stillness that no living thing could attain.

I can't recall the jumble of thoughts careening through my head. Even if I could remember, I doubt that they would make any sense to me now. I had just seen my father kill a man, and be killed himself.

I knelt there for no more than a few minutes but it felt much longer. I was alone with two dead men in the dark.

I think I was waiting for Pop to sit up and laugh and tell me it was a joke. I finally stood up and backed away until I could no longer see the bodies. I turned and ran for home.

I couldn't tell Mother what had happened. I just couldn't — it was too awful — so I told her that Pop was spending the night at the clubhouse. She expressed no surprise at that. Pop often worked late and slept in his office. The two of us ate chicken à la king and a chopped salad. I washed the dishes, Mother went to her study to read. I said nothing more about Pop.

By that time my thoughts had settled a bit, and I was thinking about what was to come. People would be searching for them. They might be looking for Rosen already, and when they found the bodies, then what? Rosen was the district attorney. They would think that Pop had attacked Rosen, and Rosen had defended himself. Even if they couldn't prove it, the scandal would destroy my father's reputation, and probably spell the end of the country club.

I know that sounds cold and calculating, especially for a seventeen-year-old kid, but those were the thoughts that ran through my mind that night. I was incapable of worrying about my mother's emotional response, let alone my own. I have since learned that that isn't uncommon. Some people respond to an emotional shock by seeking refuge in the cold-blooded minutia of survival.

Such was my mind-set when I slipped out of the house after Mother had gone to bed. I walked across the golf course to the maintenance garage where we kept an old Ford tractor with a bucket on the front and a backhoe on the back.

The moon, almost full, had risen. I could see the bodies on the sand as I drove the tractor up to the bunker. Nothing had changed. I picked up the bloodied golf club and put it in Pop's golf bag. I got back on the tractor and dug a pit in the sand next to the bodies.

Four feet down I reached a layer of peaty muck. Water seeped into the pit. The swamp Pop had drained was still there, just beneath the surface. I climbed off the tractor and rolled Rosen's body into the pit. It landed with a splash. I picked up the gun, wondering whether it was the same pistol Stan had used to shoot up that bar. I threw it on top of Rosen's body, then dragged Pop over and rolled him in too.

My plan at first had been to simply cover the bodies with sand, but I got to thinking: What if they search the golf course with dogs? Would the dogs smell the blood? Would the odor from the decomposing bodies sift up through the sand?

I drove back to the clubhouse. A year earlier Pop had built a stone patio just off the club bar on the west side. The limestone blocks he used were enormous—six feet long, three feet wide, and half a foot thick. Two of the slabs had gone unused and were stored behind the maintenance garage, covered with vines. After a bit of jockeying, I managed to get the bucket under one of the slabs. I drove the tractor back to the seventh hole with the limestone slab balanced on the bucket.

Two feet of black, swampy water had seeped into the pit from below. Only Pop's knee and one of his hands were visible. I eased the slab over the hole and slid it off. It fit perfectly. I scooped the sand back in the hole with the backhoe, then got off the tractor and used a sand rake to smooth the surface of the bunker. It looked pretty good, but there was still blood mixed in with the sand, and I was worried about dogs sniffing it out. The tractor tires had left clear marks on the grassy verge, and I was worried about that too.

As if in answer, the moonlight went away. A bank of low clouds had moved in. I saw a flicker of lightning on the western horizon. It was an answer from the heavens. A good hard rain would rinse the sand and wash away the tire marks. I felt as if my work had been blessed— by the devil, perhaps, but blessed nonetheless.

By the time I returned the tractor to the garage the rain had begun to fall. I scrubbed the blood off the golf club, put it back in the bag, and left the clubs in Pop's office where he usually kept them. The rain was coming down hard by then. I walked home across the golf course, heedless of the lightning, letting the rain run down my face and body in a cleansing torrent. I was feeling powerful, giddy almost, as if I had done a wonderful thing.

I did not think about my father or Robert Rosen or Rosen's family. I would think about those things later, but on that night I had been seized by a sort of madness. I was a young man who had accepted a role, who had completed his mission while setting aside the rightness, the wrongness, the impossibility of it all. I was a soldier who had witnessed an atrocity, and committed one of his own. I could not allow myself to think about what I was doing or what I had done.

Years later I read a book about the Nazi war criminal Adolf Eichmann, who was responsible for the deaths of millions of Jews, Poles, Hungarians, and others. The book's author used the term "the banality of evil." Eichmann had set aside his soul and done his job with emotionless, dull efficiency—not out of hatred or passion or fear, but simply because he had a job to do.

On that long night, I was Adolf Eichmann—just a soldier doing his job.

I arrived home utterly soaked. I stripped off my clothes and crawled into bed and slept until awakened by the morning sun blasting in through my window and Mother standing at the foot of my bed looking down at me.

"I can't find your father," she said.

There was more. When Stuey finally reached the end and closed the notebook it was after one in the morning. He lay back and stared at the ceiling and thought.

Things nobody knows, Gramps had said.

Things nobody would believe.

My Book of Secrets.

If they were supposed to be secrets, then why had Gramps written them down?

It's our history, Gramps had said.

It was Stuey's history too.

Stuey went to his window. The full moon lit the tops of the apple trees; the shadows beneath the branches were stark black. He could see the top of his grandfather's gravestone poking up through the tall grass.

Had anything changed?

A dark form detached itself from the shadow of the

nearest apple tree. He saw a flash of white. A face? The figure turned its back and moved off into the orchard's shadows with a familiar shuffle.

Gramps.

Stuey's neck prickled; his heart thumped. He stood at the window for a long time, but Grandpa Zach did not return.

the truth

Stuey was awakened the next morning by the doorbell. He heard his mother clomping from her studio to the front door. He looked out through his bedroom window. A dark-blue sedan was parked in the driveway—an unmarked police car like the one Detective Roode drove. He ran downstairs.

Detective Roode was standing in the foyer talking to his mom. Stuey moved closer.

"Are you sure?" his mom was saying.

"A wallet was found beneath the body," said the detective. "We were able to read his driver's license. To be absolutely certain, we will have to compare his DNA with yours, but given the estimated age of the remains and the fact that they were found on what was once your grandfather's golf course . . ."

"Where he was last seen," Stuey's mom said.

"Yes."

"I never knew him," she said.

Detective Roode nodded. "In any case, you are his closest relative. We wanted to let you know right away so that we can release the information to the public."

"So that people will stop thinking you found Elly Frankel?"

"Precisely."

"Do you know how he died?"

"That will have to wait for the autopsy," Roode said. "But we are treating this as a murder investigation. After all, he didn't bury himself." He frowned. "It was more than sixty years ago. We may never know what happened."

"It was my great-grandpa, right?" Stuey said.

They both looked at him, startled. "Where did you come from?" his mom asked.

"Is it him?" Stuey said.

Roode looked at Stuey's mom, who nodded.

"We think so," Roode said.

"What about Robert Rosen?" Stuey said.

His mom gave him a sharp look. Detective Roode leaned toward him and asked, "What did you say?"

"Didn't he disappear at the same time as my great-grandpa?"

Roode straightened and forced himself to smile. He turned to Stuey's mom and said, "Your son is correct, Mrs. Becker. We did indeed find two sets of remains, but we hope to keep that under wraps until we locate Robert Rosen's next of kin."

"You won't have to look far," she said. "Maddy Frankel is his granddaughter."

After Detective Roode left, Stuey's mom went to the sofa and sat down and said nothing. Stuey stood there watching her stare into space. After a minute he said, "Mom?"

She looked at him as if she'd forgotten he was there.

"Oh, Stuey," she said, and shook her head. "It's so sad. All those years of suspicion and blame. I suppose we'll never know what really happened."

"Maybe we will."

She frowned. "Why would you say that?"

"I'll show you." He ran upstairs and got the notebook.

"It's Gramps's *Book of Secrets*." He pushed the notebook into her hands. "I read it, so they're not secret anymore."

She held the notebook in her lap without opening it.

He said, "Remember what Gramps said about secrets?

He said secrets have the power to break the world in two. If I have a secret and you don't know it, then you live in one world and I live in another, right? And if the secret is really, really big, then maybe our worlds break apart completely."

She smiled in a puzzled sort of way. "When did you become a philosopher?"

"He also said there were ghosts."

"That was just your grandfather talking."

"I believe him."

"Stuey, honey, there are no such things as ghosts."

"Gramps said ghosts are made of memories, and he said they get stuck here because of secrets. I think Gramps got stuck. I think his dad got stuck too." He pointed at the notebook in her hands. "Aren't you going to open it?"

She shook her head and set the notebook aside.

"I've read it," she said.

"You have?"

"Daddy had it with him when he died. He was holding on to it when we found him, clutching it to his belly as if it was the most important thing in the world. I read it that night and hid it in the golf bag."

"You knew?"

"I know what Daddy wrote."

"But . . . why didn't you tell anybody? Why didn't you tell Elly's mom?"

"It happened a long time ago, Stuey. Before I was born. I just didn't see any reason to dredge up the past. I was so happy when you and Elly became such good friends. I thought we'd left our family's secrets behind."

"We have to tell," Stuey said. "We have to make the secrets not secret anymore."

She shook her head slowly. "Why? What difference could it make?"

"It could change everything!"

"Stuey . . ."

"Don't you see? The world broke apart because of secrets, and now Elly's gone and the woods are gone and maybe we can fix it!"

She put her hand on his head, as if trying to keep him from floating away. "Stuey, there is nothing we can say or do that will bring the woods back. Or Elly."

"You're wrong," he said. "We have to fix it. We can tell the police so they don't go looking for a murderer when Grandpa Ford and Robert Rosen actually killed each other. Like Gramps said—they hated each other to death. We can tell the Frankels. So they know what really happened, and when everybody knows the truth, then—"

His mom was looking at him with a pinched expression.

"I'm not crazy," he said. "I've talked to Gramps. He's the one who told me to find the notebook."

Stuey was afraid she would get mad, but she didn't. Instead, she opened the notebook and flipped slowly through the pages. After a few minutes she looked up.

"I don't know what to do," she said.

"We have to tell the truth," Stuey said.

what if

They told the truth.

Nothing changed.

What had he expected? That Castle Rose would rise up from the flattened forest? That the trees would grow back overnight? That Elly would come strolling up the driveway?

His mom made copies of Gramps's notebook. She gave one to the police and one to Maddy Frankel. Parts of it were printed in the newspaper and for a few days all of Westdale was buzzing with the old news . . . but nothing changed. It was ancient history. The mall was being built. Elly was still gone. Life in Westdale went on.

For the next few weeks, every day, Stuey visited the spot where the Castle Rose had stood. It was marked by the broken limestone slab and a slight depression where the stone had been. A few torn strips of yellow police tape were strewn about.

Elly never showed up.

In August the men came with their big machines, bringing truckloads of gravel, concrete, and stone blocks. Soon, the mall began to rise where once there had been a forest.

Mr. and Mrs. Frankel sold their house and moved to Atlanta.

School started again.

Time passed.

I write these words now looking out my window at the forest that was once my father's country club, and I think how the golf course devoured the marsh, and how my father and Robert Rosen devoured each other, and how my actions devoured the truth.

I have lived my life with this secret, a veil of darkness that separates me from everyone else in the world, and I wonder how things might have been different. What if Pop had never drained the marsh to build his golf course? Or if he had not gone out onto the golf course that night? Or if Robert Rosen had not followed him?

If Pop hadn't swung that golf club at Rosen, would Rosen have fired his gun? If Rosen hadn't threatened Pop with the gun, would Pop have swung the club? And what if I had not buried the bodies? What if I had called the police and told them what I had seen? Each of those acts would have led to a different future, a different reality.

Is reality simply a dream we share? Will sharing my story change what is real? Alas, I will never know.

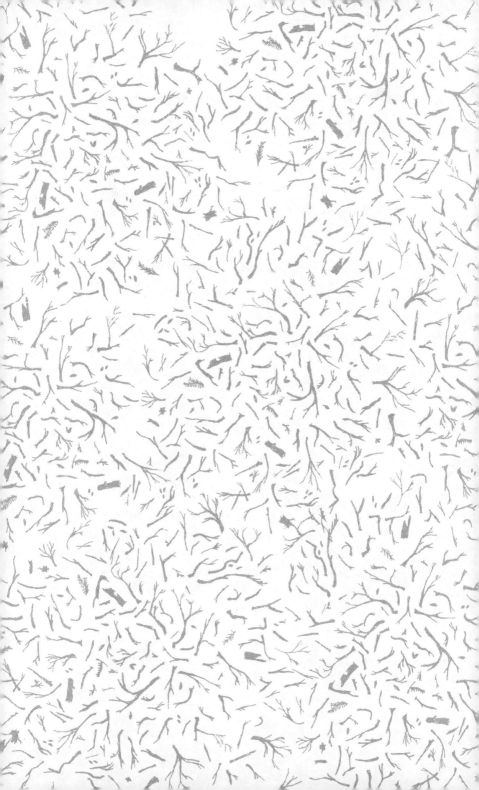

thirteen

birthdays

"Elenora!"

Elly groaned and ground her face into her pillow.

"Elenora Rose! It's a quarter to seven!" The voice sliced down the hall and through her door and jabbed into her ears. She turned her face toward the clock next to her bed. It was only 6:36.

"You lie," she mumbled.

"Elenora Rose Frankel! I want to hear you in that shower this minute!"

She sat up and rubbed her eyes with her palms.

"Elenora!"

She shoved her covers aside, swung her legs off the bed.

"Elenora!"

She stomped down the hall to the bathroom, making sure she was heard. She turned on the shower and sat down on the toilet and stared at the multicolored floor tiles. Sometimes she could make the tile pattern look like flowers, but this morning it looked like random rectangles, hard and cold beneath her bare feet. A single dark hair had appeared on top of her left big toe. She pinched it between her nails and yanked it off. Stupid hair.

She let the shower run for another minute, then turned it off. She leaned over the sink and splashed some water on her face. She dragged her fingers through her thick, insanely curly black hair and risked a quick glance in the mirror. Same stupid pointy face. She turned her head so she could see the streak of blue she'd dyed into it, and she smiled. Her mom hated that blue streak. She turned away from her reflection, stripped off the shorts and tank top she had slept in, and got dressed. Clean underwear from the laundry basket. Jeans from yesterday. A random T-shirt. Was it dance class day, or pottery day? Every morning it was something, even in the middle of summer. She looked down at her shirt, at a chocolate stain that hadn't quite come out in the wash, and hoped it was pottery day. The stain wouldn't matter then.

"Elenora!"

She left her nightclothes on the bathroom floor and

shuffled zombie style toward the kitchen. The table was set for her, as always: a bowl, a carton of milk, a box of granola, and half a grapefruit. One thing was different this morning. On a small plate next to the grapefruit was a small cherry tart with a candle stuck in it.

Her mother said, "Happy thirteenth birthday, Elly Rose."

Because it was her birthday, Elly declared, she wouldn't go to dance class or whatever she was supposed to do.

"Don't you want to see your friends?" her mom said.

"I don't have any friends."

"What are you going to do then? Sit around the house and mope?"

"I'm going out on the lake."

"You spend more time in that kayak than you do at home!"

Elly didn't bother to reply.

"Don't forget to put on sunscreen," her mom said.

On the morning of his thirteenth birthday, Stuey's mom gave him a hundred-dollar Mall Pass—a gift certificate good at any store at Southdale, a mall fifteen miles away.

"You can use it to buy yourself new school clothes," she said.

"Mom, school doesn't start for two months!"

"It's just a suggestion," she said. "You can buy whatever you want."

"But this certificate is for *Southdale*. How am I supposed to get there?"

"I'll drive you there this weekend." She pointed in the direction of the Macy's building looming over the treetops. "I'm not giving one nickel to that eyesore!"

"Whatever," Stuey said. "I'm going over there now."

"You spend too much time in that place."

"You used to tell me I spent too much time in the woods."

"Right, and the woods are gone."

"Anyways, thanks for the gift certificate."

"You're welcome."

Stuey went up to his room to get his baseball cap and his wallet. He only had four dollars. He rooted through his drawers, looking for change. He found two quarters, a nickel—and the compass. He hadn't looked at it since the last time he'd seen Elly—the time he'd gotten soaked. The bezel was rusty, the glass was clouded, and the needle was frozen. He held it tight in his hand, feeling a hollowness grow inside his chest. He started to put it back in the drawer, then changed his mind and hung it around his neck.

"Happy birthday, Elly Rose," he said.

no mushrooms

Through the orchard, past the poplar grove, and over the knoll. How many times had he walked that path? He squeezed through a cut he'd made in the chain-link fence and scrambled down the steep bank to the parking lot of Westdale Mall.

The mall had turned out to be even bigger than Stuey had imagined. It took them a year and a half to build it. There was an enormous Macy's at one end and a Super-Target at the other. In between were sixty-two smaller stores, a Life Time Fitness, three restaurants, a twelve-screen theater, and a huge semicircular food court selling everything from pizza slices to sushi.

The mall curved around a pond. They called it West-dale Lake, even though it was so small you could throw a rock across it. A fringe of trees separated the surrounding parking lots from the neighborhoods on each side.

The mall had been open since last fall. Stuey went there a few times a week, because with the woods gone, there was nothing else to do within walking distance, and it was a place he could hang out with his friends.

"Hey, Stu! Wait up!"

Stuey looked over his shoulder. Deshan and Alison. Alison was swinging an Old Navy shopping bag. Deshan had his Bait Bag.

"Any bites?" Stuey asked him.

Deshan shrugged. "Nah, man, they're on to me. They hardly ever check it anymore. I could steal 'em blind if I wanted."

"What do you have in there today?" Stuey asked.

Alison made a disgusted face. "It's really gross."

"Nah it ain't," Deshan said. "Just some old socks."

"Yeah, off your stinky feet."

"My feet are not stinky," Deshan said. "They're *aromatic.*"

Deshan had been bringing his Bait Bag to the mall for half the summer. Last spring the security guards at Macy's had hauled him into their back room, questioned him for an hour, and rooted through the contents of his backpack. They didn't find anything except some books, a water bottle, and his phone. It happened again a week later at the Hobby Stop. Deshan declared that enough was enough.

"It's 'cause I'm black," he had said. "You know it is."

He was right. More than once, Stuey had seen Deshan get hassled by the mall cops and store security. They all got hassled a little bit because they were teenagers, but Deshan got way more than his share. A few weeks earlier he had dubbed his backpack the Bait Bag, and every time he went to the mall he filled it with things like rotten fruit, used tissues, crumpled fast-food bags, and now dirty laundry. According to Deshan, the best moment ever was when a security lady from Verona's Closet reached in and encountered one of his dog's poop bags. Deshan's dog was a Saint Bernard.

"They know me now," Deshan said. "It's no fun anymore."

"So what are you guys doing?" Stuey asked.

"Cineplex marathon," Alison said.

"Yeah, one kissing movie and two where they blow things up," Deshan said. "I won the coin flip. You in?"

"Nah, I'm just gonna hang," Stuey said. He didn't want to admit that he only had four and a half dollars. Also, he'd feel like a third wheel. He was good friends with both Alison and Deshan, but when it was the three of them together he felt like an accessory.

"Cool. Whatever. Catch you later."

Stuey watched them go, feeling a little left out. Maybe he'd run into somebody he knew at the food court.

It was only 11:30. The food court was dead—just a few people who worked at the mall and a handful of middle-aged shoppers. Stuey bought a slice of pizza from Sbarro even though he wasn't that hungry. He sat down at a table that gave him a good view of the whole court so he could watch the people passing by.

This was once a forest, he thought. As near as he could figure out, he was sitting close to where the deadfall had been. The food court was his new Castle Rose. Instead of cherry pie, he was eating pizza.

He examined his slice. Pepperoni, some crumbles of Italian sausage, sliced mushrooms, green pepper, olives, and some flecks that might have been basil. He picked off the mushrooms, because that's what Elly would have done, and it was her birthday too.

But Elly wasn't there. It had been two years ago today that Castle Rose was destroyed. Two years since their great-grandfathers' bodies were unearthed. He'd seen her for just a few seconds that day, and he'd gotten soaking wet, but nothing since.

Had any of it really happened?

Gramps had written, *Is reality simply a dream we share?* If so, then what reality was this? Was eating pizza in this food court as real as sitting on the slab of rock in Castle Rose?

He pulled the compass out and turned it so the frozen needle pointed north. There had been a time when he thought it was magic. So stupid.

He took a bite of the pizza and chewed thoughtfully. It had been four years since Elly disappeared, and he had only known her for a month or so. Just a tiny slice of his life. Why did he think about her so much? Had they really been soul mates? Was that even really a thing? Maybe they were just two lonely kids who got thrown together.

The compass needle trembled.

"Happy birthday!"

Stuey jerked his head up. Elly was sitting across from him, smiling.

the food court

Elly had changed. Her face wasn't so thin. Her hair was down past her shoulders, with a corkscrew streak of bright blue from her forehead all the way to the ends of her curls. She had a nose ring.

"It's not real," she said.

"You're not really here?"

"The nose ring. It's fake. You should've seen my mom's face when I came home with it. It was hilarious."

"I like your hair."

"That freaked her out too. You look good. You're taller. Where are you?"

"In the food court at the mall."

"They really built it then?"

"Yeah. It's huge. There are, like, fifty stores here. There's a store that sells nothing but refrigerator magnets. Where are you?"

"I'm on Westdale Lake."

"Lake?"

"Yeah, they flooded part of the woods two years ago. I'm in my kayak. Can you feel it?"

He *could* feel it, as if his chair was gently rising, falling, rocking on the water.

"You're sitting on the end," she said. "Your feet are in the water. Don't make any sudden moves or you'll tip us over. We're floating over Castle Rose. I'm holding on to a branch that's sticking up out of the water. Hey, I can smell your pizza!"

"My feet are wet," Stuey said, looking under the table.

"Can I have some?"

He passed the slice to her and watched her take a bite. It was weird how they had just started talking like they always had, as if they'd never been apart.

"Thanks for taking off the mushrooms," she said.

"That's okay. It's your birthday."

"So what's new? I mean, I know you have a mall instead of a lake, but do you have a girlfriend?"

Stuey thought about Alison. "I have a friend who's a girl, but she's not my girlfriend."

"What's her name?"

"Alison."

"Alison Quist?"

Stuey gaped at her. "How did you know?"

"There's only one Alison our age in school."

"She's more like Deshan's girlfriend."

"I know Deshan. He's friends with Heck Hellman."

"Same here."

"Heck got kicked out of school for smoking."

"Really?" Stuey had never seen Heck smoke. Apparently some things besides the mall and the lake were different in their worlds. "I thought your parents sent you to Atlanta."

"Just one year. I kicked up a fuss and now I go to school here."

Stuey shook his head. "It's not fair. There gets to be two each of Alison and Heck and Deshan but only one of each of us."

"It's totally unacceptable." They looked across the table at each other, both of them grinning. "I wish I could come hang out with you at the mall."

"That's kind of what we're doing."

"Except I'm on a boat, and you're sitting at a table with wet feet." She ate another bite of pizza.

"You can have the rest of it," Stuey said. "I'm not all that hungry."

"I bet I'm the first person ever to eat hot pizza in a kayak in the middle of a lake."

"And I'm the first person to sit on a kayak in the middle of a food court."

"My mom thinks I'm insane," Elly said. "I used to wonder that myself."

"But you don't now?"

She shrugged. "You have to admit, if this is real, it's kind of . . . unreal."

"My grandpa said that reality is just all of us having the same dream. We have a two-person reality."

"I wish we could agree on a reality where we could live in the same world."

"Me too."

She noticed the compass. "You still have it! Do you wear it all the time?"

"I think it's broken. I don't really need it because there's no woods to get lost in anymore."

"Maybe it's what keeps us connected."

"Maybe," Stuey said. "But I think it's mostly because we're like two pieces of a puzzle that fit together. Except the connection broke because of secrets."

"What secrets?"

"My grandfather's secrets."

"What does that have to do with *us*?"

"In your world the Castle Rose is under a lake, but in my world they tore it down. They lifted up the rock where we used to sit. You remember how it would move, and we could hear voices sometimes?",

Elly nodded.

"There were bones under the rock. At first they thought they were your bones, but there were two skeletons, and they were really old."

Elly was breathing fast, the way she had the day he told her about their great-grandfathers.

"I found Gramps's *Book of Secrets*," he said, speaking quickly because he was afraid she'd disappear again. "My mom hid it in the pocket of his golf bag. It tells what happened. You have to read it."

"Can't you just tell me?" Her voice sounded small and distant, and she was looking blurry.

"Go to my house." His voice rose to a shout. "It's in Gramps's room! In the pocket of his golf bag! Go!"

A hand clapped down on his shoulder, and she was gone.

"Elly!" he shouted. "Elly!"

"Son!"

Stuey looked up into the broad, mustached face of a mall security guard.

"Who are you yelling at?" the mall cop asked.

Stuey was breathing hard.

"Are you on drugs, son?"

Stuey shook his head.

"You better calm down and move on, son," the mall cop said.

"I'm fine. I was just—"

"Move along, son."

clogs

One moment Stuey was sitting on the end of her kayak, and then he wasn't. The bow popped up as his weight left it. There was no splash, no falling into the lake—he simply evaporated. The kayak bobbed on the water's surface. Elly sat for a time, trying to make sense of it. She could still taste the pizza.

Go to my house, he had told her.

Elly didn't want to. She was afraid. The last time she'd gone there Stuey's mom had been so scary. But she had to go.

She dipped one end of the paddle into the water and stroked. The kayak moved away from the deadhead. She paddled toward Stuey's side of the lake. The stand of poplars that had once surrounded the fairy circle stood naked near the shore, water lapping at their pale trunks. She guided the kayak through the poplars and wedged it into a thicket of honeysuckle and climbed out.

She crossed the meadow to the orchard. The trees were loaded with tiny green apples. Buckthorn and nettles filled the spaces between the trees. The orchard was becoming part of the woods.

She weaved her way through the trees. The house came into view. The lawn was nearly as overgrown as the orchard. Mrs. Becker's car, parked in the weedy, crumbling asphalt driveway, had two flat tires. Elly took a deep breath and approached the front door.

Now what? Knock? *Excuse me, Mrs. Becker? I was wondering if I could see your father's old bedroom so I can steal his notebook?*

She didn't think that would work.

Elly continued around the house and peered through a window looking into the kitchen. The sink was piled high with dirty dishes. She went to the next window, a sitting room that looked like no one had sat in it in years. Another window looked in on Mrs. Becker's studio. A half-finished painting of a robin sat propped on an easel. The table beside it was covered with dried-up paints and brushes.

Elly moved from window to window but saw no sign that anyone was home.

The back door was unlocked. She pulled it open slowly, wincing at the groan of rusting hinges. The small mudroom was full of dusty old flowerpots, gardening tools, and stale air. She listened. Nothing.

The mudroom led into the kitchen, which was even messier than it had looked from outside and reeked of old garbage. On the table was an open jar of peanut butter, a box of Ritz crackers, and a teacup with a drying tea bag next to it. She crept through the kitchen to the hallway leading to the living room. A curving staircase led to the upper floors.

Again, she stopped and listened. If Stuey's mom was home she was being very quiet. Maybe she was sleeping.

Elly knew that Stuey's grandfather's old room was on the second floor at the end of the hall, right under Stuey's bedroom. She climbed the stairs slowly, keeping to the outside of the steps to avoid creaking. At the landing she looked each way. To her left there was a short hallway with a door on each side. On her right was a longer hallway, with four doors. One of the doors stood open. She edged up to the open door and peeked inside. It was a bedroom. The covers were thrown back and lay in a tangle at the foot of the bed. Clothes were strewn on the floor. Glasses and plates were piled on the nightstand.

Elly moved past the room and approached the door at the end of the hall. She turned the knob and pushed the door open.

Inside, the room was a blur. At first she didn't know what she was looking at, then she realized the room was filled with spiderwebs from floor to ceiling. It looked like stringy fog.

Clunk-ka-clunk. Clunk-ka-clunk. Clunk-ka-clunk.

Mrs. Becker was coming down from the third floor, her clogs clunking on the steps. Elly didn't want to face her—she could never explain what she was doing there. She took a deep breath, stepped into the webbing, and quietly closed the door.

Clunk-ka-clunk-ka-clunk-ka-clunk . . . The sound got louder, then faded as Stuey's mom descended to the first floor.

Elly breathed shallowly through her nose. Her arms and face tickled unpleasantly from the hundreds of fine strands of sticky webbing. She waved her arms, making a space for herself. Wispy strands hung from her hands and forearms. She didn't see any spiders, but that didn't mean they weren't there.

The center of the room wasn't so bad—most of the cobwebs were along the walls. She looked around at the things Stuey's grandfather had left behind: the sword, the books, the photos, and a wooden stand holding several oddly carved pipes. There was a cardboard box full of moldy yellow papers on the bed. Leaning against the wall in the corner was an old leather golf bag. She brushed away the cobwebs and unzipped the side pocket.

There it was. The notebook. Just as Stuey had said it would be. She opened it and read a few lines.

Clunk-ka-clunk, clunk-ka-clunk . . .

Mrs. Becker was coming back up the stairs.

Clunk-ka-clunk, clunk-ka-clunk . . .

The sound lessened—she was going up to the third floor. Elly opened the door and peeked out. The hallway was empty.

Carrying the notebook, she crept down the stairway to the kitchen and let herself out the back door. She ran across the yard. As she entered the orchard she tripped and fell headlong. The notebook flew from her hands. She climbed to her feet and looked back at what had tripped her. Stuey's grandfather's gravestone. The notebook had landed a few yards away in the tall grasses. Elly grabbed it and glanced back at the house.

From the third-floor window—Stuey's bedroom—Mrs. Becker was staring out at her, haggard and ghostly pale.

Elly ran. She ran through the orchard and the meadow to where her kayak waited. She jumped in and paddled out onto the lake, not stopping or looking back until she reached the deadhead.

"Stuey?" Her voice seemed small. There was no response. She stared at the bow of the kayak, willing him to appear as he had before.

Nothing.

She looked back toward shore, half expecting Mrs. Becker to be standing there, but saw only the ring of dead poplar trees. After a time, she opened the notebook and began to read.

two malls

Elly closed the notebook. Her stomach was a knot. Her brain felt as if it wanted to burst out of her skull. She shuddered at the thought of the hours she had spent in Castle Rose, of the voices she and Stuey had heard, of the day the slab had grabbed her and tried to pull her down into the earth. She thought about the angry scarecrow man in the suit. Had that been her great-grandfather? He *had* looked a bit like her uncle Rob.

She imagined the two dead men twined together for decades, still arguing, still hating each other.

And now? They were still down there, directly beneath her, under the water, under the slab. Were they still fighting?

She pushed away from the deadhead with her paddle. Strange—the deadhead was sticking up higher than she remembered. She started to turn the kayak, then stopped. Her mouth fell open. Something was wrong. The shoreline had gotten closer. The poplar grove was now on dry land. She spun the kayak. The wooded hillside to the east looked bigger—the water didn't rise up quite so high. The lake had shrunk. Were they draining it? She looked to the north, toward the Barnett Creek inlet.

A long, low building, like a small shopping center, stood between the lake and the highway.

But that was *wrong*. That land was part of Westdale Wood. The building hadn't been there this morning. It hadn't been there an hour ago.

It was impossible.

Stuey wandered through the mall, not really looking at anything, just thinking about Elly, trying to understand what had happened. She'd said that in her world there was no mall, and the woods had been flooded to make a lake. In Elly's world, Castle Rose was underwater.

Was there a copy of Gramps's notebook in her world? Would she find it? What would happen when she read it? Would anything change?

He walked past the food court. The mall cop was still there. Stuey wanted to get back to his table in case Elly came back, but he knew if the security guy saw him he'd be asked to leave again. Especially since he didn't have enough money left to buy anything.

Another circuit through the west wing, past the Gap, Godiva Chocolatier, Aeropostale, Starbucks . . . He spotted a quarter on the floor and scooped it up. With the change from his pizza purchase he had ninety-four cents. Was there anything he could buy for that in the food court? If he bought something, maybe the cop would let him sit at the table again.

The mall cop was still in the food court, chatting with a girl working at Cinnabon. Stuey looked over the menu boards. The least expensive thing he could find was a small soft drink for ninety-nine cents, a buck seven with tax. He wandered back through the mall, keeping his eyes on the floor for loose bits of change. A nickel in front of the refrigerator magnet shop. Three pennies under the tables in the atrium. A dime next to a potted palm tree.

He counted his stash. One dollar and twelve cents. He started back toward the food court, then stopped, confused. Somehow he had wandered into an unfamiliar part of the mall. That was odd. He knew the entire mall inside and out. But he was standing in front of a shop he'd never seen before called Dollyworld. The display window was full of oversize dolls. An older woman was adjusting the jumper of a four-foot-tall rag doll set up just outside the shop doors.

"Excuse me," Stuey said. "How long has this store been here?"

The woman smiled and tipped her head. "We've always been here," she said. "At least since the mall opened."

"Oh. I never noticed it before."

"Do you like dolls?"

"Um, not really." Stuey looked up and down the corridor. "Which way is the food court?"

"Food court?" She laughed. "I suppose you could call it that." She pointed to her right. "It's not as if you could get lost in here!"

"Thanks," Stuey said, and set off. He walked past three more stores he'd never seen before: a place that sold cell phones, a women's shoe store, and a jeweler. The mall seemed miniature, with narrower corridors and a lower ceiling than he remembered. The corridor ended in an area with a few tables and chairs, a Subway sandwich shop, and a Dairy Queen. Another, smaller food court? Since when?

One side of the food court was all windows looking out on a patio with two picnic tables. On the other side of the patio was a strip of grass, and beyond that a lake.

But there was no lake anywhere near Westdale Mall, just a little pond. Was he dreaming? Had he sleepwalked to some other mall miles away? His heart was pounding.

"Better close your mouth, kid, or you're gonna catch a fly in there."

Stuey whirled. The man who had spoken was sitting at one of the tables eating a vanilla cone. He looked eerily familiar.

"You look like you've seen a ghost," the man said, and Stuey suddenly recognized him. It was the Mushroom Man—Greg Eagen—but he was dressed in jeans and a polo shirt, and he had shaved off his beard.

The man took a lick of his cone, then frowned and asked, "You okay, kid?"

"My name's not kid. It's Stuey."

"Is that a fact? Nice to meet you, Stuey."

"You don't remember me?"

The man shook his head.

"You saved me when I got stuck in the deadfall."

"Deadfall? Sorry." Clearly, he didn't remember Stuey at all.

"You're the mushroom guy, right?"

"How do you know I'm interested in mushrooms?"

"Because—" Stuey looked past him, out the windows at the lake, and saw something that made him stop breathing. The Mushroom Man started to say something but Stuey was running out the doors. He ran across the patio and the grass to the edge of the lake.

Out in the middle of the lake, a dark-haired girl in a red kayak was paddling toward him.

gravestones

Elly let the kayak drift the last few yards to the shore. Neither of them spoke. He reached down and grabbed the front of the kayak and pulled it up onto the grass.

"Well," she said, "I'm here." She looked scared.

Stuey nodded.

"In your world," she said.

"No."

"No?"

"This is a different world," he said. "This isn't the right mall—it's like a mini-mall. And we don't have a lake like this, just a pond."

"We don't have any mall at all," Elly said. She climbed out of the kayak. "And my lake is bigger."

They looked at each other.

"Then where are we?" Stuey asked.

Elly thought for a moment, then said, "Someplace different. But this building—I feel like I've seen it before." She looked out across the lake. "There are more woods." She pointed. "You can see where the fairy circle is. It's above water now."

"Did you get the notebook? Did you read it?"

Elly nodded.

"Did you see my mom?"

"Yes."

"Is she okay?"

Elly hesitated, then said, "No."

"I'm sure she'll be okay once she sees you," Elly said.

They were walking through the woods along the north side of the lake. Elly had been telling Stuey about his mom—how her place was falling apart and how she'd turned into some sort of hermit. Stuey kept walking faster. Elly had to run to catch up. At the top of the oak knoll she grabbed his arm.

"Stuey, wait!"

He stopped.

"We'll get there," Elly said.

Stuey closed his eyes and nodded shakily. He looked around, seeming to realize where he was for the first time.

"They cut this hill in half and put a fence up," he said. "From here to the other side is all parking lots and stores. I mean, it was."

"Maybe it still is. In the other world."

"You mean there's still a world with me in it, and a different world with just you?"

"Unless we stuck them back together."

"But if we didn't, does that mean that there's still a place with just you, and another place with just me?"

"Maybe we both disappeared from both places," Elly said.

"But there are two Alisons, and two Hecks, and two Deshans, right? And two of my mom. So maybe there's more than one of us. Maybe it's like my grandpa said: an infinity of realities."

"That makes my brain hurt."

They descended the knoll and soon came to the fairy circle. It had grown smaller—the poplars were marching in on the creepy bent.

"I'm scared," Stuey said. "What if she doesn't remember me? What if she isn't even there? What if she's moved away? Or dead or something?"

"I'm scared too. You said my parents were going to move away."

"They did move. To Atlanta."

"No!"

"But everything is different here. I bet they're still here. We can go see them next."

They crossed the meadow and entered the orchard. The grass had been cut. The apple trees stood out in neat rows.

"This morning this was all overgrown." Elly pointed through the trees at the house. "Look! It's painted white! It was gray before, right?"

Stuey wasn't looking at the house. He was staring at something that sent a shiver up his spine. He took a step. His legs went weak and he dropped to his knees.

"Stuey?" Elly grabbed his arm. "What's wrong?"

Stuey pointed a shaking finger.

Where Gramps's grave had been, there were two headstones.

Elly helped him up. Stuey managed to move forward, each step slower than the last. After what felt like an eternity, they reached the pair of headstones. Stuey tried to read what was carved on them, but he couldn't make sense of the letters.

"It's not your mom," Elly said.

The words swam into focus. The stone on the left read:

ZACHARY JOHN FORD

1934 – 2014

He forced himself to read the name on the other gravestone.

STUART GILES FORD

1905 – 1951

party

"Who is Stuart Giles Ford?" Elly asked.

"It's my great-grandfather." He couldn't stop staring at the headstone. "But what's he doing here?"

"Isn't this your family graveyard?"

"Yeah, but before there was just Gramps."

"Really?" Elly looked puzzled. "I thought there were always two gravestones."

"You did? But . . ." The funny thing was, as soon as she said it, Stuey remembered two gravestones too. Except, at the same time, he remembered there had been only one.

"Your yard looks nice. I thought it was all over-grown . . ." Elly looked toward the house. "I don't know why I thought your house used to be gray. It was always white, wasn't it?"

"I think we painted it white after Gramps died, but . . . it's like I remember it both ways."

"Your mom's car was different."

The car parked in the driveway was a little red hybrid, shiny and new.

"It had two flat tires," she said. "It was blue."

"We used to have a blue car," Stuey said. "Mom must've got a new one." As soon as he spoke those words he remembered her buying the red Prius last year. "I think I'm remembering things I didn't remember before."

"Me too. Like, I remember a world where you were gone. But I remember this world too, just like we were always here."

"Maybe we *were* always here."

"There's your mom."

Stuey's mom was coming around the corner from the front yard. Stuey started toward her, walking at first, then running. She looked up, startled, and caught him as he threw himself into her arms.

"Whoa!" she said. She held him at arm's length. "What was that for?"

"I'm just glad to see you're okay," Stuey said.

"Of course I'm okay!" She looked past him. "Hey, Elly Rose. I thought you'd be coming with your mom."

"My mom?" Elly looked confused, then her expression cleared and she said, "Oh. Yeah. I decided to kayak over to the mall."

"That silly little mall." Stuey's mom shook her head. "I don't know why you kids spend so much time there." She sighed. "I guess a few shops is better than that megamonstrosity they were threatening to build." A car turned into the driveway. "Here's your mom now."

The car pulled up next to the house. Mrs. Frankel got out.

"I see my kayak girl made it on time," she said with a red-lipsticked smile.

Elly ran to her and hugged her, just like Stuey had with his mom.

Stuey asked, "Mom, when did great-grandpa Stuart get his own gravestone?"

She gave him a puzzled look. "You don't remember?"

"I was trying to remember if it was before or after Gramps died."

"It was right after Daddy passed. Remember we found his notebook?"

Memories swirled and collided in Stuey's head, and suddenly he *did* remember. "Oh. Yeah. It was kind of a big deal. There were reporters and stuff."

"Such a terrible thing, but at the same time it was a relief to finally know the truth. It took the police a week to find them under that big pile of dead trees. When we were finally able to claim my grandfather's remains, we buried him right next to Grandpa Zach. The Frankels buried Maddy's grandfather at Westlawn Cemetery."

"Was she mad at us?" Stuey asked.

"Maddy? Not at all. She was relieved to know the truth about what happened." She looked over at Elly and her mother, and she smiled. "Our grandfathers were mortal enemies, and yet Maddy and I have become the best of friends."

Elly and her mom were coming toward them. Mrs. Frankel was carrying two round plastic containers.

"What do you have there, Maddy?" Stuey's mom asked.

"Pies. Our cherries ripened early this year."

"Mom makes the best cherry pie," Elly said.

"Nothing but the best for my birthday girl!"

Stuey had completely forgotten it was his and Elly's birthday.

"Come on inside, Maddy," Stuey's mom said. "I could use a hand with the salads. The others will be here soon." The two women headed into the house.

Stuey and Elly looked at each other.

"Others?" Stuey said.

Elly pointed toward the front yard, where there was

a grill, two coolers, and a long picnic table topped with covered bowls, paper plates, and plastic glasses. "I think we're having a birthday party."

"Oh. Yeah. I remember now."

"You do?"

"Our moms have been planning this for weeks."

"Everything's changing," Elly said.

"I know! Our moms are friends now."

"Your mom seems good."

"She was really upset when they tore down the whole woods . . . except they didn't! There's plenty of woods left, and we have a lake."

"I thought the lake was bigger. I thought you were gone."

"There was a giant ugly mall, and you were gone too." Even as he spoke, his memory of the gigantic mall became fuzzy and indistinct. "Are we forgetting old stuff, or remembering new stuff?"

"I don't know."

Another car turned into the driveway. "That's my dad," Elly said, waving.

A minute later, Heck rode in on his BMX. He skidded to a stop in front of Stuey and said, "Is Deshan coming?"

"I don't know," Stuey said, then remembered inviting him. "I think so."

"Cool. Where's the grindage?" *Grindage* was Heck's word for food.

Stuey pointed toward the picnic table.

Heck dumped his bike on the lawn. A moment later he was tearing into a bag of chips.

"He likes to eat," Stuey observed.

"No kidding," Elly said. "Here comes Jenny." Jenny Garner's mom was dropping her off at the end of the driveway. "I think I was mad at her, but now I can't remember why."

"Maybe that's good. I think I'm forgetting some bad stuff too."

Elly nodded thoughtfully. "You told me something about a gigantic mall."

"I remember telling you that, but when I try to remember the mall it gets all fuzzy. I remember these huge buildings, and then I see the little strip mall and the big buildings sort of fade away, like remembering a dream. Was I telling you a dream?"

"I don't know. Hey, who's that?"

Another car had pulled in. A tall man and a kid with long black hair got out and walked toward them. They looked familiar, but Stuey couldn't place them. The man was smiling; the kid looked nervous.

"Are you Stuey?" the man asked.

Stuey nodded.

The kid was staring at him through strands of hair. He stuck out his hand.

"Hey," he said.

Stuey shook his hand. "Er . . . hey?"

"You don't remember me?" The kid smiled shyly. "I'm Jack. Jack Kopishke."

cherry pie

Fifteen people showed up for the party. The biggest surprise was Jack, Stuey's best friend from when he was seven years old. Stuey's mom had arranged to have Jack's dad drive him up from Des Moines just for the party. It had been six years. It was great to see him again, but they didn't talk long—all Jack wanted to talk about was *World of Warcraft*. Stuey introduced him to Heck, who was also a hard-core gamer, and those two got along great.

It was a good party. There was one kid Stuey didn't recognize at first, but as soon as he started talking to him, he realized it was Danny Lee, who had moved in two houses down a year ago after the Kimballs left the neighborhood. How had he forgotten Danny? They were good friends.

There were lots of presents—mostly gift cards. Jack Kopishke gave him a *Black Ops* baseball cap. Elly got a friendship bracelet from Jenny Garner. Mr. Frankel cooked burgers and bratwursts. There was fruit salad, his mom's vegetarian baked beans, a monstrous tray of nachos brought by Danny Lee's mother, and all sorts of junk food.

And, of course, cherry pie.

While Mrs. Frankel was serving wedges of pie, Elly caught Stuey's eye and jerked her head toward the back door. They slipped out through the mudroom and took their pie out to the orchard and sat on the grass in front of the gravestones.

"I can't believe I forgot there were two graves," Stuey said.

"We forgot forks," Elly said.

It sounded like something she had said before, but Stuey couldn't remember when.

"I feel like we've done this," Elly said.

"We have?" Stuey thought back. It was an effort, as if he had to force his way through a forest of memories. "We were in a place."

"Was it a castle?"

"I barely remember it."

Elly grabbed his hands. "We can't forget!"

"Gramps once told me that there are different realities, but we can only know the one we're in."

"Remember the time you hit your head falling off the swing?"

Memories flickered, faded, solidified. "I crashed my bike."

"Oh." Elly blinked confusedly. "I thought I remembered a swing . . . no, you're right. You were on your bike. I gave you a compass."

"You did?"

"It's around your neck!"

Stuey felt his neck. There was a chain. He pulled it out. Attached to the chain was a smooth red stone with a hole in it.

"You gave me this," he said.

"Oh!" She laughed. "Of course! I gave it to you the day you fell off your bike. I thought it was like a magic amulet or something. I can't believe you still have it."

Stuey rubbed the stone between his fingers, feeling the familiar, comforting smoothness of it. "I suppose if we forget stuff we'll never know we forgot it, because we won't remember." He looked down at his slice of pie on its paper plate. "How are we going to eat this?"

Elly picked up her slice with both hands and shoved the pointed end in her mouth. Stuey did the same. His teeth sank into the cherry filling and his mouth exploded with flavors. It was perfectly sweet, perfectly tart, and the flaky, buttery crust was the best he'd ever had. He swallowed and said, "Wow!"

Elly grinned and licked a glob of cherry from the corner of her mouth. "My mom makes the *best* cherry pie."

Stuey took another bite. Even better.

He had never tasted anything like it.

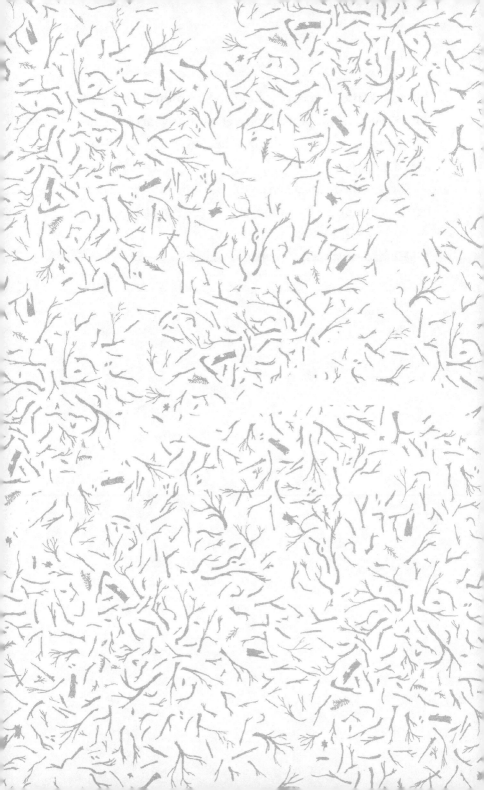

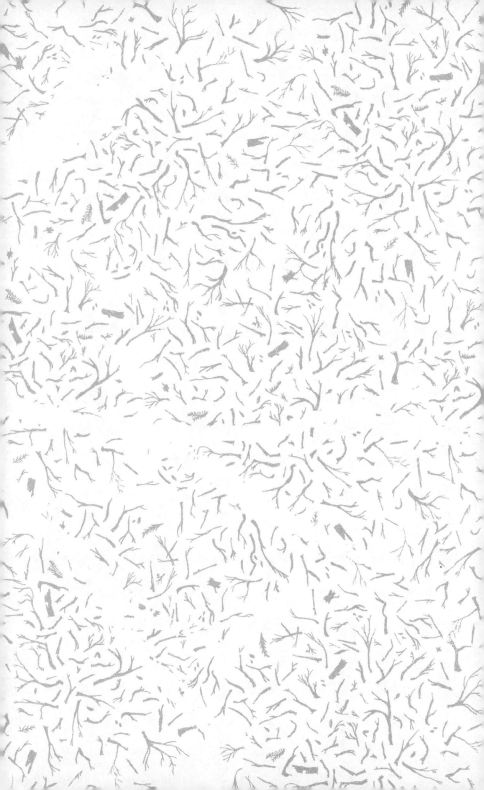

afterword

I grew up on a dead-end street with a forest behind our house—a large wooded area that had once been a golf course. I remember my dad taking me for that first walk in the woods. I was five years old. He taught me the names of the trees and the animals. He taught me about poison ivy and wild berries. We discovered a patch of creeping bent, all that remained of the old golf course.

Those woods became my playground, my refuge, my universe. I swung across a ravine on a grapevine swing, and spent many hours playing inside a deadfall fort. I sank to my knees in a peat bog, suffered countless mosquito bites and nettle stings, and built memories that will be with me to the end of my life. When I was ten years old, part of the woods was flooded by a nearby creek. It became a hundred-acre, deadhead-studded lake, perfect for rafting in the summer and ice-skating in the winter.

Today, a third of the old woods has been leveled to make room for auto dealerships and office buildings. The rest has been preserved as a nature center. It's no longer the wild place I remember — there are fences and wood-chip trails, interpretive signage and rules. I still go there a few times a year to search out the old paths and reawaken memories, but it is not the same. The magic is still there, but it has become civilized and lethargic. *Otherwood* is my eulogy to the woods that live now only in my memory.

acknowledgments

I did not write this book alone. Mary Logue read several versions, and always guided me back to the story when I became lost in the woods. Thank you, Mary. My childhood friend Leslie Harris, who grew up on the other side of the woods, helped me find the heart of the story — I don't always know what my books are really about, you see. Thank you, Leslie. Thank you to my siblings, who helped prop up my memories. And finally, thanks to my editor, Katie Cunningham, and the entire team at Candlewick Press — you make our dreams reality.